MIRROR WITCH MAGIC

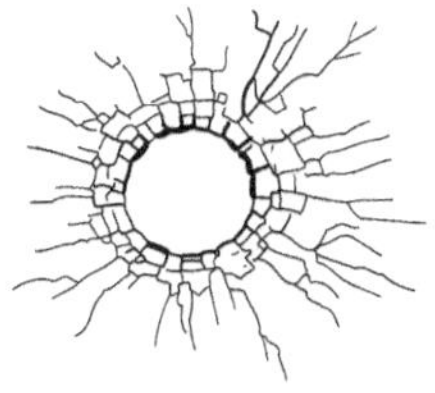

*S**ome secrets stay buried while others surface just like the dead.***

Fusion City—a place where magic was power and the more a person had, the higher up the caste system they went. It was also the perfect place for Selena Decland, a mirror witch wanting to shuck the responsibility of her magic and lineage, to fly under the radar. At least it was until someone left a dead body on her nightclub's steps, along with a note written in blood:

I know your secret.

As Selena struggled to keep her secret hidden, she is faced with threats from multiple places—a rep from the witch's council who would like nothing better than to sell Selena's talents to the highest bidder; a powerful demon who could make life difficult if he found out her secret; and a killer willing to do anything, including use dark magic, to get what he wants.

Contents

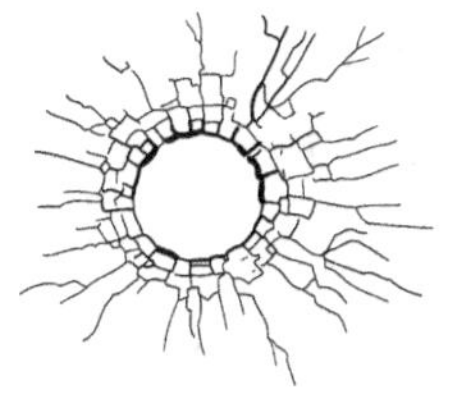

Chapter 1

Magic. It pulsed, danced, and tangled with every beat of the music pumping through the club. Selena stood on the upper level of her nightclub looking down at the patrons, lost in the moment. She shifted, one hand resting on the rail and the other playing with the necklace around her neck. The polygon-shaped pendant was made up of small mirrors and matched her dress perfectly. The fitted top pushed up her cleavage while the loose fabric fell to mid-thigh, shifting and sliding like mercury as she moved down the stairs to the lower level.

Selena loved observing them, the partygoers who came to Valaria to let go and find their deepest desires. Everyone had a desire, a need they couldn't always get met in the actual world. Only at Valaria could they get those needs fulfilled. Well, at least temporarily. That it wasn't permanent didn't stop droves of beings from coming to her club and throwing down credits to have their dreams come true, even for one night. The corner of her mouth tilted up as a group of fauns toasted each other.

Purple mist rose from their cups, and they knocked back the potion like a shot, the mist escaping on their breaths. In seconds, a flash of light burst from the chest of each faun, showering them in magical flowers. Others oohed and aahed at the falling petals that caressed the drinkers' skin before being absorbed. Wherever it touched, the fawns changed form. The earthly creatures of fur, hooves, and horns became different. One with less magic but with enough power to keep the rest of the magical world under their thumb. A human.

"A potion for your thoughts?" The hand that held the cedar goblet in front of her was as honeyed as the voice. Selena stared into the almond-shaped and colored eyes of her six-foot-tall potion master and best friend. He flipped his pin-straight blue hair, exposing the shaved side of his scalp along with a trio of rings in his ear. His eyes were the picture of innocence as she scowled. "What are you trying to get me to do this time—fall in love or go out on a blind date?"

Shalik lifted his right hand to his chest. "I swear I'm not trying to get you to fall in love or do anything nefarious."

She gave him another suspicious look, but took the cup from his hand and knocked back the contents much like the fawns had.

"Humm, this one's superb." She eyed him over the cup. "What does this one do?"

He tilted his head, his hair shifting past his shoulders. "Besides taste delicious?" She rolled her eyes. "It has the daily serving of vegetables you need."

She groaned. "Why do you keep insisting that I consume those things? They're horrible. Grown in the depths of the Abyss by Abaddon himself."

He shook his head. "I doubt Abaddon, ruler of the Abyss, has the time to grow vegetables just to punish people."

"You'd be surprised," she mumbled.

He folded his arms over his chest.

"Whatever." She handed him back the empty goblet before turning back to the fauns, who were now fully human and out on the dance floor having the time of their lives. "By the way, the flowers were a nice touch. It certainly attracted a lot of attention. Word's going to spread about that one."

His grin was devilish. "I aim to please, master."

Selena sucked her teeth. "How long are you going to harp on me about this?"

"Until you admit you're as much as a softy as I am, and that's why you signed the papers to be my little protege's master."

She scoffed. "I signed the damn papers because I knew if I didn't, you'd moping around here, making my life a level of the Abyss and giving me calf eyes."

"Sure," he said, his grin widening.

"Just you watch—I'm going back to the prefecture office tomorrow to return those papers and get a refund." She huffed when Shalik laughed. "Laugh it up, blue boy. I'm returning yours, too."

He laughed even harder, wiping the tears from his eyes. "I'd like to see you try to run this place without me, doll." He flicked her nose, then sashayed over to stand behind the bar and deposit her empty cup. She followed, sliding onto a barstool and propping her elbow on the slick marble surface.

"Speaking of your protege, how's he doing?" she asked.

"See for yourself." Shalik jerked his head to a cluster of witches. They tossed sparkling dust that cascaded down and settled on their skin, causing it to glow the way a higher-level witch's would at the height of her power. Selena supposed their dream was to see what they would look like if they ever came into their full powers. A common-enough request from a witch—why be anything else when one could be at the top of the food chain in Fusion City?

She faced her potion master again. "He did an excellent job, very advanced for a beginner."

He grinned, drying the goblet he'd washed when she wasn't paying attention. "I told you from the beginning that he had potential."

"Yeah, maybe I'll ditch you for him, so I won't have to put up with all the attitude."

Shalik flicked her nose again. "One of these days, that smart mouth is going to get you into trouble."

"Well, isn't that the cauldron calling the wood black?"

"Whatever, smart ass. Come dance with me," he said, walking around the bar to take her hand and to lead her onto the dance floor.

She tugged her hand away. "You go ahead. I'm not in the mood."

Shalik frowned. "What's wrong?"

"Nothing, I just don't feel like the workout tonight." She knew her response was lame, but she couldn't explain the feeling she'd had since leaving their upstairs apartment.

Shalik stood with one hip cocked, waiting her out.

"Fine. I feel like someone's watching me," she mumbled.

Shalik smiled. "Of course they're watching you." He grasped her hand, tugging her off the stool before turning her to face one of the many mirrors in the room. "Have you seen yourself? You look amazing. Your outfit suits everything about you, including your magic."

She forced a grin. "It was a magnificent find, wasn't it?"

Shalik wrapped his arms around her from the back, then rested his chin on top of her head. "Yup. I'm sure they're wondering if you're the resurrected soul of the mirror witch even more now."

Shalik made an *umph* sound when Selena's elbow connected with his ribs. He stepped back with a grin, rubbing the offending spot.

"Don't give the eavesdropping patrons any ideas," she snapped.

"Oh, come on. Everyone here knows you don't have the power to give them more magic—not *permanently*. Just relax and come out on the dance floor."

Selena caved, allowing him to lead her to the floor. She smiled when he engulfed her in his arms, letting the music move her with each pounding beat. All the while, she fought the gut-twisting feeling that someone evil was watching her.

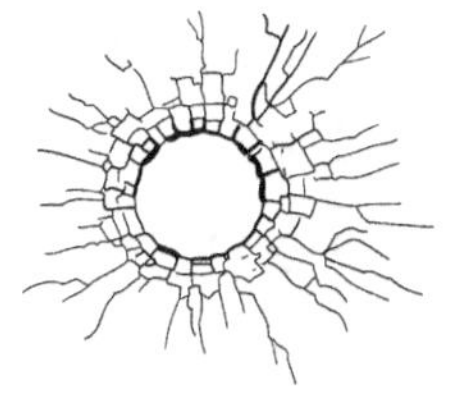

Chapter 2

"Cerberus!" Selena screamed, waving a partially chewed-up shoe from the doorway of her walk-in closet. The guilty party who'd committed the heinous crime remained hidden somewhere in the sprawling four-bedroom penthouse apartment. "Don't even think about hiding. Get out here this instant."

Selena heard a guilty whine. She marched barefooted to where the mutt hid. When she'd gotten to the other side of the couch, she saw that his nose was stuck under the edge of the sofa. His butt vibrated as he tried to dislodge himself.

"I should leave you there as punishment," she muttered, lifting the corner. The dog scrambled back from where he tried to hide from her displeasure. He plopped onto his butt, giving her puppy-dog eyes. "Don't look at me like that. Look what you did to my brand-new Hamumara shoe." She waved the chewed-up remnants of her designer shoe she'd worn only once. He whined again, covering his face with a paw. "I've told you a million times not to eat my shoes!"

Just then, the front door opened. Shalik walked in, closing it behind him. His keys clanked as he dropped them in the bowl she'd left on the small table by the door. "What's going on?"

Selena waved the evidence of Cerberus' crimes in the air, and Shalik winced. "Is that the one you paid nine hundred credits to have custom made?" Her answering growl was affirmation enough. He held up his hands in an 'I surrender' gesture. "Why don't I take Cer out for a walk, so you can finish getting ready for your big meeting? I assume you'll have to change outfits because you don't have shoes to match?"

Selena let out a thin scream as she stomped back to her closet. She heard Shalik whispering to Cerberus on their way out. "Now, why did you have to chew up Mommy's shoes on a day like this?" The dog gave one sharp bark, and Selena opted to tune them out until they were out the door.

She took a deep breath to calm her nerves, then pulled out her backup suit with the matching shoes. Today, she was heading to the Salva building at the center of Fusion City to renew her club's license. For every other being in this entire city, it was a matter of filling out a form and mailing it in. But for her, a mirror witch, it was a full-out court case. She had to go before the Council to prove she had enough power to warrant a business, plus sufficient control over her magic to keep patrons safe. For her, she had to prove that the fun times she provided hundreds of patrons weren't causing permanent damage. To everyone in the city, it looked like the Council was taking precautions and protecting everyone, but Selena knew the truth. It was all a crock of shit. She was being treated this way because she had mirror witch powers, and the one witch on the Council wanted Selena to be something she was not.

She changed into the new suit, a navy affair with a short skirt and matching jacket she paired with a white shirt. The new shoes were identical to the suit's color, with a white stripe near the front. Grabbing her white briefcase with the gold loop handles, she headed out the door to the elevator. She was out the private entrance in a matter of minutes. Her feet clacked on the smooth sidewalk as she headed into the heart of Fusion City. Various being bustled about their business, ignoring everyone, or filled with too much self-importance to notice anything else. Gods, she loved this city. The crush of people she was constantly surrounded by, yet still oddly managed to feel alone. It was one of the major reasons she'd stayed when she'd come years ago. She could observe and not be a part of the social standing that made up Fusion City.

A pixie shouted curses at a taxi driver for almost running him over at the crosswalk, and Selena grinned. Others gathered in long lines to grab a cup of coffee, even though two blocks down, there was another coffee shop from the same chain. Even more humans and magic workers stood in the shade of skyscrapers, hunched over their phones or chatting with others about the latest celebrity news or work woes.

Fusion City was just what the name implied—a melting pot of beings crammed into one place. She stood by the corner, waiting for the light to change before crossing and heading deeper into the city's center. Who'd have thought after a millennium in the shadows for fear of death, this multitude of magical beings would thrive in the light? Although the fear still hung in the balance, it only came from the Council now. They ruled all supernatural beings at the humans' behest, aka the supernatural middlemen. It turned out that if one were supernatural and not part of their boot-licking club, then they made one's life a living level of the Abyss. The only thing that made them slightly cooperative was money and power. It was lucky Selena had enough credits to make the Council toe the line. But every few years, she still had to dance through hoops just because they felt the need to remind her that she was under their laws.

The sharp ring of a bell was her only sign that a bike messenger was approaching.

"Watch it," she shouted as the fawn sped past her, almost clipping her with his handles. She watched him ride off, oblivious to the angry screams left in his wake. She turned to continue her walk to the Salva building when she caught a shadow of movement out of her peripheral vision. A sliver of cold crept up her spine, and she fought off a shiver. Turning slowly, she searched the tree-lined walkway for anything that could have caused the morbid feeling, but nothing stood out. Everyone went about their day, studiously ignoring her the way only a Fusion City native could do.

She gave herself an inner shake as she continued toward the center of Mid-park, where the building stood in all its blinding white, pretentious glory. A reminder to all lesser beings on who held the power over them. Selena scoffed—as if taxes, fees, and regulated slavery weren't enough of a reminder. Taking a deep breath, she forced herself to exhale the tension that built whenever she thought about this topic. She couldn't afford to get worked up over something she couldn't change. If she went in there with her temper blazing, she might lose her club's license, which would bring on an entirely different set of problems.

Squaring her shoulders, she climbed the steps and prepared to face the Council's dooming presence.

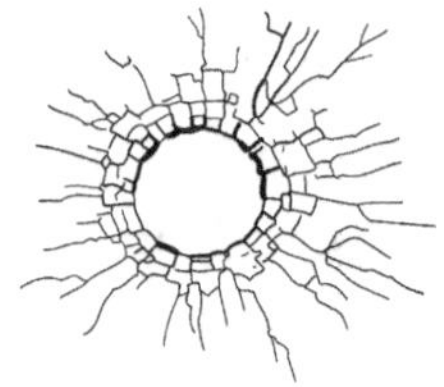

Chapter 3

The building that housed the Council was not only white outside but also inside as well. They specifically chose the color to signify the purity and unity represented by the Council—if one believed all the PR bullshit they tried to sell. The truth was, it was just like any other government building. It took hours to get things done. There was always way too much paperwork for a building that used magic, and the seating in the anti-chamber was designed by someone who would make a large sum of credits if they worked in the Abyss.

Selena shifted once more as the unyielding surface of the bench bit into her lower back and ass, numbing all feeling. Gods, she hated coming to this bloody place, hated they made people wait as a form of intimidation even though they already knew whether they would permit what someone wanted before they stepped through the door.

And boy, did they make her wait—an extra hour past her appointment time. She sat, eyes closed and head leaned back with legs outstretched. She looked the picture of relaxed when she actually felt like she was sitting in a light bulb. All the damn white on white was giving her a blinding headache to the point of nausea, but she sat still, calm breaths going in and out for the cameras watching her. Selena couldn't figure out why they would use something reflective to spy on a mirror witch. Obviously, she could sense that it was there. Did they think her power was so low she wouldn't know?

She took in another breath and let it out slowly, still the picture of ease. After another half hour, she decided enough was enough. Sending a tendril of her magic out, she cracked every camera lens in the anti-chamber, never lifting a finger or varying her breaths. Five minutes later, the clipped sound of heels on the tile punctuated the Council attendant's steps like an exclamation. Selena kept her hands clasped over her stomach as the sound halted next to her.

Someone cleared their throat, but she still refused to open her eyes or move.

"Ms. Decland?" The name was said like a question, but Selena wasn't sure what the woman was asking. Opening her eyes slowly to avoid being blinded by all the white, she stared up at a familiar face. The right corner of Selena's lips tilted in amusement.

"Ms. Decland?" Selena asked. "Why so formal, Minerver?" Her amusement grew as Minerver Pinkerton placed one tanned hand on the hip of her powder-blue suit and tapped the matching high heel against the floor.

"Must you be so difficult?" she huffed.

Selena grinned. "How am I difficult? I'm just sitting here, hours past my appointment time, to see the illustrious Council members."

Minerver shook her head. "If you would just cooperate with the Council and take the Hyōka to see what level your magic is, things would go much smoother for you. They wouldn't doubt your abilities to run your club."

All amusement died from Selena at her old friend's statement. Eyes hard, she rose slowly to her feet. "Not everyone wants to be the Council's pet, Minerver."

Minerver sighed. "Why do you always have to be so defensive about everything? I'm just trying to help you."

"If you want to help, then convince the Council to stop treating lower-level beings as indentured slaves," Selena said through gritted teeth.

Minerver tucked an imaginary stray hair back with the other curls she'd brushed into submission and twisted into a bun. "They're not slaves, Lena. Like everyone else, they need to work to ensure the collective stays sufficiently funded to survive."

"After all these years, I can't believe you're still spewing this bullshit, Mini." Selena tossed her head, the curls she'd twisted away from her face bouncing around her shoulders. "You and I both know it's just a way for the Council to remind the lower-powered beings of their places and to get enough money to appease the human taxes. Without cheap and talented labor, many of the upper levels wouldn't be able to run their business and make a profit."

"Businesses like yours?" Minerver smirked. "I heard you indentured another potion master. Business must be doing well."

"Yes, it is, actually, and Shalik asked for someone new to train. You remember Shalik, right? His indentured service will be completed soon. He'll be free, and he'll have enough money to live a very lavish lifestyle. What about you, Mini? How long before you're able to move up the ranks in the Council's maze?"

Selena watched as the barb hit home and Minerver's face blanked.

"Despite everything, Selena, I want the best for all beings in Fusion City. Even though you may disagree, the Council is working to make things better for everyone."

Selena scoffed.

"If that's all you have to say, I'll show you to the Council." Turning, Minerver headed for the door on the opposite end of the exit.

Selena followed without another word, walking past Miniver into the Council room, the doors closing behind her. The color scheme here continued in all white, except for the high division bench that housed the three Council members. The human, the witch, and the demon—the three members who were supposed to represent all the beings in Fusion City. To Selena, it felt like these three were the most powerful and took advantage of any being who wasn't stronger than them. There was no voice to represent the fauns, pixies, sprites, lower-level witches, or any of the hundreds of other beings.

Knowing the drill, Selena walked to the single chair in the center of the room and waited. She kept her face blank as she focused on the high division bench they sat upon.

"Ms. Decland, you may sit." The deep, sensual voice, let her know it was the demon who'd spoken. Since her early arrival to Fusion City, she'd known Raesean, Abaddon's second, general of the Abyss armies. Everything about him garnered the attention of every female within a five-mile radius, including her. But she knew better than anyone never to trust a demon. They were always after their own agenda. It was why she'd avoided him as much as possible. This, of course, he met with so much amusement and challenge that Selena was forced to ignore him every time they came into contact.

Taking a seat on the old high-backed chair, she planted her bag on her lap and gazed at the Council, barely keeping herself from rolling her eyes. The human was on his phone texting or playing some game. He didn't even acknowledge her. The demon was dressed in his signature designer dark suit that fit him so well it had to be custom made. His slicked-back white hair stopped at the nape of his neck, his alabaster skin shining. As he lounged in his chair, he kept his glacial-blue eyes on her, never wavering as though he was committing everything about her to memory. Even back when she, Mini, Shalik, and Lucien used to frequent his club, Raesean had kept his eye on her—whether he suspected something or she was just a fascinating challenge, Selena couldn't tell.

Shifting, she finally turned her gaze to the bane of her existence—Ofilia Hart. The highest-powered mirrored witch known. Unfortunately, her power level was one point shy of being high-tiered. A fact that probably chapped her ass regularly. It was also why she was always behind Selena to get tested—to prove once and for all who had the highest power levels and might gain the reincarnated mirror witch powers the prophecy spoke about.

A prophecy that had Selena avoiding testing like the plague. Since the beginning of witches, it was said that every half-century, a mirror witch born with a high-power level would come into her full abilities. She would possess one of the highest powers a mirror witch could have. Each of the previously documented witches could harvest the sun's power, make portals, or reveal the truth. The only other power left was the ability to do magic transference—the ability to capture someone's magic using a mirror and transfer it to another being.

Despite Selena's many protests, many believed she could be the mirror witch because her power level was undocumented. More than anything, every lesser being wanted her to give them more power. To take from the rich and give to the poor. Unfortunately, Selena wasn't up for living life on a pedestal. She enjoyed being able to live freely away from anyone's expectations. It was why she'd come to Fusion City. Well, at least that was what she told herself.

Selena's magic ran to darker tastes. If anyone found out, they would either try to weaponise her or burn her at the stake.

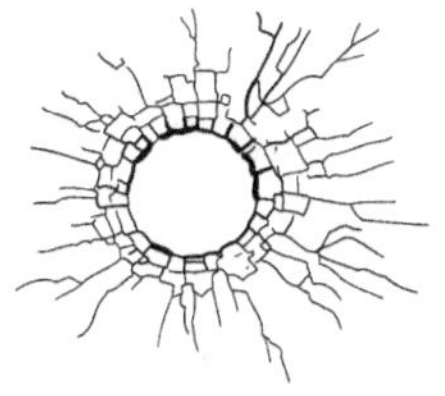

Chapter 4

"**M**s. Decland, you're here to renew your business license?" Ofilia gave her a pointed look from her seat on the Council bench. Her hair was pulled back in its usual merciless bun, and she wore no makeup. Her powder-blue robes were the exact color of Mini's suit. Rumor had it Ofilia made everyone who worked for her wear the color, a subtle reminder to others of who she was. Selena rolled her eyes at the thought.

"Ms. Decland?" Ofilia said, bringing Selena's attention back to her question.

"I believe," Selena said with a huff. "That's what it says on the paperwork you each have a copy of."

Ofilia glared. "A simple yes or no would suffice."

"Yes."

"And can you tell us more about the type of business you're running?" she asked.

Selena took a breath. All this information was on the forms she filled out in triplicate before coming to this meeting. They were also questions the Council already knew the answers to. Apparently, Ofilia was on a mission to waste her time today.

"I run a nightclub," Selena grumbled.

"But not just a regular nightclub," Raesean interjected. "You run a magical nightclub that grants people's desires and keeps demons out. A feat most average witches or demons can't accomplish."

Selena shrugged.

"Yes, Ms. Decland." Ofilia leaned forward in her seat. "Tell us how you can do this with what you claim is merely average powers."

Selena huffed out an impatient breath. "I told you, Ofilia, the reincarnated powers of a high-level mirror witch won't come to me. My powers are average as indicated on the migration papers I filled out when I came to Fusion City."

"So you've said. Yet, here you are, accomplishing high-level magic such as keeping demons out of your club."

Selena closed her eyes, fighting the building anger that prickled her skin like needles. "My power lies in desire. I put a spell on my club's mirrors that allow patrons to enter if their desires are happy with no ill intent. That demons can't enter the club is an indication that their desires lean toward darker needs and have nothing to do with my magic."

"Interesting..." Raesean said

"So, you don't have a spell to keep demons out specifically?" Ofilia pressed.

"No, I can't prevent any particular race of beings from entering my club. Besides, that would be racist and also illegal in Fusion City if I'm not mistaken."

A snore came from the human, and Selena glanced over at the man. He'd propped his foot up, leaned back in his chair, and fallen asleep.

Selena was sure the disgust in Raesean's face reflected her own. Ofilia hadn't bothered with taking her eyes off Selena. She was hunting for information, and she was locked onto her prey until she had it.

"I suppose your inability to prevent certain beings from entering your club is why you took out a restraining order on your ex-boyfriend. Lucien, I believe, is his name."

Selena sucked in a breath. "What does that have to do with anything?"

Ofilia's smile was dark as she responded. "If you can't keep one little pixie from entering your club without the help of enforcers, then how do I—*we*—know you can protect the innocent patrons of your club? I mean, can you, with your supposedly meager magic, tell if someone is using dark magic in your club? Can you tell if someone is using magic for ill purposes?"

After all the hours of waiting in uncomfortable silence, her heated discussion with Mini, and now this bullshit with Ofilia, Selena's temper frayed.

"Look, Ofilia," she snapped, her magic beginning to build. "Any witch worth their salt could sense dark magic. If you ask the other Council members, you'd know I've spent enough time in the lower westside to be able to do so."

Ofilia waved her hand in dismissal, and the last string of Selena's temper snap. Her power surged, and her skin glowed. The overhead lights flickered and sparked, causing some bulbs to go out.

"Selena," Raesean shouted. Her gaze snapped to his, and their eyes locked. It was enough to remind her about where she was. When he frowned, she took a deep breath, forcing her magic back. She shifted her gaze to Ofilia, staring the woman down.

"Seems as though you were right, Selena. Your power is nowhere near the high level I thought it would be if such a paltry display is all you can put on."

Selena smiled. "Oh, I thought that was you," she responded. "After all, I don't have the power to do such things. I only deal with desire. I suppose if you think it paltry, you would know best."

The remainder of the bulbs shattered. Except, it wasn't Selena's magic causing it this time. The pair of mirror witches glared at each other as glass rained down, each using their power to prevent it from falling on them.

"Ladies," Raesean snapped. They looked at him. "I think it's best we wrapped this up." He shook out the glass from the file folder he'd used as a mini umbrella. The seat next to him where the human sat had been vacated some time during

Selena's showdown with Ofilia. The room was now lit by the emergency lights that glowed a garish red.

Selena was done with the charade. "Are you going to renew my license? If not, then I'm sure I could peddle my services privately."

Ofilia stared at her, probably weighing the option of losing the fee money over being vindictive.

"Three years," she said.

"What? I was told I could get five because I have a higher income bracket."

"Three years, and you're on probation. If anything goes wrong at your club, then we reserve the right to pull your license." Ofilia smirked, and Selena glared.

"Fine," she gritted out. Without another word, she stood and stomped out of the Council room.

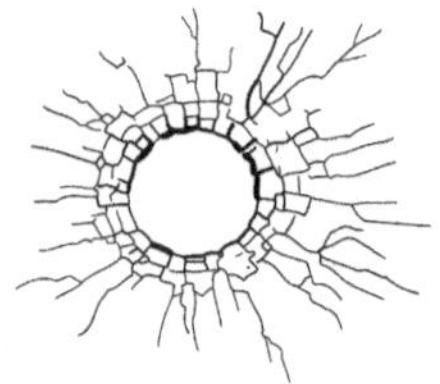

Chapter 5

S elena curled her feet under her on the sofa as she shoveled another spoonful of cherry-coconut ice cream into her mouth. She paid no attention to the indistinct murmurs of the news anchors talking about the sudden increase of missing beings in Fusion City. After the day she'd had, the last thing she wanted to dwell on was more bad news. The lock on the front door tumbled, and she didn't bother to look up from her next spoonful. The sharp barking and the scratching of nails on the foyer tiles let her know Shalik was back from babysitting the mutt and running errands. Cerberus scrabbled around the sofa, then took a giant leap up next to her. He didn't waste any time wiggling onto her lap, trying to lick her face in apology for this morning's activities.

"All right, all right," she said, giggling at the furry bundle. She placed the almost-empty bowl on the black coffee table. Before the dog got any ideas about sharing, she scratched him under the chin. He collapsed unto his back, limbs splayed, as though encouraging her to continue rubbing past his chin to his stomach. She shook her head as she obliged him.

"Oh, oh..." Shalik's voice had her glancing up. He picked up the remains of her swiftly melting ice cream before dropping down on the other end of the sofa, taking a spoonful, before giving her a rueful look. If anyone knew how much it took out of her to deal with the Council, it was him.

"On a scale of 'you never have to see them again' to 'we have to close the business,' how bad is it?" His eyes were worried and with good reason. If she lost the business, then she would lose all rights to his indentured papers. He would have to seek indentureship elsewhere. If he were lucky, his next master would allow him to finish the two years he had remaining, but, in most cases, they would force him to start a new one. She reached over to pat him on the thigh.

"Not as bad as the business closing. Let's face it—they love the money I bring in too much."

"But..." he prompted, knowing her well enough to tell there was more she hadn't said.

"I got into it with Ofilia."

He dropped the spoon back into the bowl, his eyes sliding shut. "Shit."

"I know I shouldn't have..."

"You can't keep letting her get under your skin, Lena. Once she knows she's getting to you, she's just going to dig in and keep at it."

"I know, damn it." Selena stood, shifting the comatose Cerberus to the floor. She needed to pace. All the anger she felt had yet to dissipate under her onslaught of ice cream, so she used movement to rid her of the rest. "I was already so riled up after seeing bloody Miniver that Ofilia just pushed all my buttons, and I lost it."

"Mini was there? Why?" his head tilted to the side as though trying to work out a particularly hard puzzle.

"What do you mean why?" Selena stood, hands on her hips and bare feet planted firmly. She'd abandoned her suit jacket and shoes somewhere when she came in. Now she looked like a white-and-navy frazzled pixie, hair escaping the front twists she'd had it in this morning, amber eyes fired up. Shalik would have teased her if the conversation wasn't so serious.

"Mini doesn't work in greetings anymore. She's been promoted to Ofilia's personal assistant."

"What?" Her mouth fell open. "When did this happen?"

"About six... no, maybe eight months ago." He shrugged as though it were nothing, but Selena knew Miniver had hurt them both when she'd taken a job with the Council. The only difference was that Shalik suffered in silence, whereas Selena just wanted Mini to suffer. Realization dawned.

"Ofilia planted her there to get a rise out of me before I went in to meet the Council."

Shalik's silence was confirmation enough, and Selena swore, rich and long.

"Feel better now?" He scratched Cerberus, who had bellied over to him, on the head.

She plopped onto the sofa next to him, energy spent. "I could throttle both for that shit."

"I know, but at least you don't have to see either for another five years."

Selena looked away from him.

"You did get another five years, didn't you?" he demanded. She held up three fingers, and he sighed. "Well, it could be worse. We'll deal with it when the time comes."

She nodded, leaning over to place her head on his shoulder. "I'm so tired of this, Li."

"You and me both, love. You and me both." He planted a kissed on the top of her head. They sat in companionable silence, letting go of the stress of the day. In the silence, the sound of shattering glass filtered in, and Selena's magic thrummed in response.

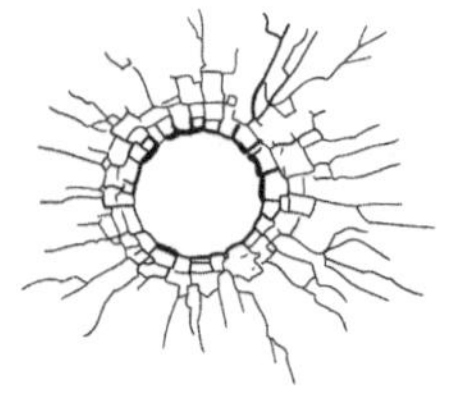

Chapter 6

Selena didn't need to guess where the broken glass was. Her magic pulled her toward it, a cord linked to a source deep within her. With Shalik hot on her heels, they stormed out of her penthouse apartment and took the elevator down to the third level of the building, where the club began. With his long legs, Shalik passed her, leaping over stairs two and three at a time until he got to the ground floor. He paused, waiting for her to catch up before they hurried to the main entrance. The pair froze.

"What the fuck?" Selena demanded.

The mirrored doors lay in pieces all over the floor of the vestibule and partly into the club. Someone had shattered them, probably using the large brick she spotted amongst all the jagged pieces of glass.

She took a step forward, but Shalik grabbed her arm, halting her steps. He pointed at her bare feet. "Shit," she muttered.

"Let me take a look," he said, picking his way through the debris. "Then you can call the enforcers."

"Okay." She shifted from foot to foot, eager to investigate herself. "I need to find the key to remove the spell. Just in case the person who did this took a piece of the mirror with them."

He nodded. "Can you feel which piece it's on?"

"Yes, it's closest to the left door," she said, pointing in the direction she could feel the spell originating from.

With quick steps, he moved to where she pointed. "This one?" he asked, picking up a large shard.

"No, it's... This is ridiculous." She sucked her teeth and took a deep breath, calming her agitation least her magic be influenced by her mood. Stretching her hands forward, she slowly opened the metaphorical fist around the magic inside herself. Directing it to her palm, she used it to clear a narrow path between the fragments from where she stood, through the vestibule, and to the main doors. When she finished, she looked up at Shalik with a grin as the euphoria hit her.

His face scolded back.

"I thought we agreed you were only going to use your magic to do mirror spells?"

"Yes, we did, with the exceptions of emergencies, and this was an emergency." She huffed, walking through the cleared path she'd made. "I wasn't about to play 'find the missing puzzle piece' with you and what looked like hundreds of pieces of broken glass." Squatting, she picked up the glass with the key. With a finger on it, she sent out a pulse of magic through the key piece down all the magical connecting cords to the other pieces, dissipating the spell of desire. With the spell removed, she stood, looking around at the mess.

"Why would anyone do this?" she demanded.

"I don't know," Shalik responded with a shrug. "Maybe someone didn't enjoy finding out what their true desire was."

"That's stupid. Breaking my mirrors won't change the outcome of their desires, and it's not my fault they wanted it."

His face looked as confused as she felt. "Who knows, maybe it was some idle kids on a dare or something."

She sighed. "If it is, I hope when the enforcers catch up to them, I get the chance to whip their hides." Selena frowned as she took in the closed main doors. "How did they get past the front door? It would have been locked."

Shalik walked the four steps across the vestibule to the double doors, then tried the left handle. It swung open with a light tug. "I know we locked up last night like we always do."

"Yes, we did, but I suppose if someone wanted to get in, they could find the means."

She moved toward him, eyes still scanning the broken glass. Once she'd reached him, she pulled both doors fully open and stared out.

She heard Shalik's sharp intake of breath long before her eyes registered what she was seeing. The body was naked and beaten so badly it was just a lump of meat. His eyes were open—one missing from the socket while the other gazed into nothingness. Broken bones jutted through his skin in various places, and the blood he'd lost pooled under him in a dark red stain on the lowest steps. On the step above him, using his blood, someone had written four words.

I know your secret.

Selena blinked in shock, taking in the horror before her, her mind trying to piece together that the body before her had once been a living being. Then the smell hit her. The scent of blood and fresh meat forced its aroma up her nose, crystallizing the reality before her, twisting the contents of her stomach.

Unable to take it anymore, she shuffled back through the club's doors, turned, and emptied her stomach.

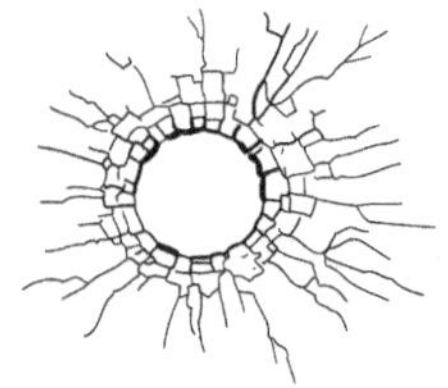

Chapter 7

Selena clutched the roughly spun blanket tighter around her bare shoulders. She hardly noted the sandpaper-like material against her skin, nor that it smelled vaguely of the healing center's chemicals used to sanitize it. No, all she could think about was the body that had laid on the steps to her club, their home, reduced to a piece of meat just to send her a message. The mystics who'd come with the enforcers to retrieve the body had taken one look at her, wrapped her in the blanket, and said she was in shock. She just sat there in silence while they'd gone about quarantining the area with red tape. Red like the blood now staining the steps. Her stomach rolled again as memories of what she'd seen assailed her.

"Selena..." Shalik's voice had her swallowing back the bile that threatened to return. As though underwater, she turned her head toward him. He'd squatted so they could be eye level, holding a short glass half-filled with a dark amber liquid.

"Drink this, love. You'll feel better." She didn't even have the presence of mind to question the contents. She just knocked it back, coughing as the liquid burned going down.

"Jeez, Li, what in the Abyss was that?" she asked between coughs.

"A little bit of this and that with a whole lot of whiskey." The side of his mouth tilted up slightly as though he wanted to smile, but after the evening's events, he couldn't. "Feelin' any better?"

She nodded slowly, then leaned forward, resting her head on his shoulder. "Who would do this, Li?"

He placed a hand on her head, running them over the mass of curls that had lost all its moisture in the day's heat and was now standing in every direction it could go. "I don't know, Lena, but, hopefully, the enforcers will find out who and why. Do you want to talk to them here, or do you want to have a seat inside the club?"

She raised her head, glancing around as though she were seeing where she was for the first time. Enforcers milled around, scanning, dusting, and gathering evidence. Most of the black tile in the vestibule, which was previously covered in glass, was now clean since the crime scene team had already collected the shards. "Yeah, I should head inside and get out of these people's way."

Shalik just nodded. He rose and pulled her to her feet, then led her to the enforcer waiting to question her.

* * *

Draykon sat at one of the club tables, observing the witch and her potion master as they navigated their way over to him. He knew who they were. One would have to be living under a rock in order not to know about the owner of the hottest nightclub in town. There wasn't a night when Fusion City citizens didn't flock to Valaria to find out their hearts' desires. When they had, the potion master was there to grant them their wishes—well, temporarily at least. He also knew some patrons who wanted to enter but couldn't. If their hearts' desires weren't happy, the mirrored doors wouldn't open to let them in. In other words, no dark wishes were allowed when one stepped into the vestibule, something the demons of the city learned the hard way. The system was ingenious, creating a haven for the partygoers and the people who worked there.

Giving himself an inner shake, he turned his thoughts back to the pair almost to the table. Barely five feet, Selena Decland was a contained spitfire with a mass of wild dark curls, copper skin that glowed under the club's lights, and a toned body with hips and legs that would cause even a dead man to raise an eyebrow. In contrast, her potion master was over six feet tall, with pin-straight blue hair, and a love of leather pants. His potions' sweetness matched his honeyed skin, and, as manager of the club, he kept the ship running smoothly.

They stopped at the table, and Selena released the death grip she had on Shalik to take a careful seat at one of the three chairs. The potion master took off to do other things.

Draykon cleared his throat. "I know this must be hard for you," he began, his tone brisk. "But I need to ask you a few questions."

She nodded. "I understand."

"Can you walk me through what happened?"

She recounted what happened right up until the enforces arrived.

He flipped back a few more pages on the notepad he had in front of him, consulting the information he had there. "Were you and the deceased personally involved at any time recently?"

"How would I know?" she snapped. "I don't even know who he is."

Draykon leaned back in his chair, tapping his pen on the open pages of the pad. "The body was right there. Didn't you look at his face?"

Magic crackled.

He could feel it building as the surrounding air tightened. He kept his eyes on the nightclub owner, watching in fascination as it shimmered over her skin. Her body turned fluid as her eyes slowly changed, the mercury color bleeding over her irises and turning them a reflective silver.

He whistled, lifting a brow. "I guess the rumors are true. You're a genuine mirror witch. Are you the five-hundred-year rarity?"

She lifted her hand, no doubt to unleash her magic, when the potion master appeared and wrapped his fingers around her wrist.

"I wouldn't provoke her if I were you." He kept his grip on her while he lowered the tray of drinks to the table with his other arm. "She's churned up, and her magic will lash out."

Dray smirked. "Your magic that unstable that you'll accidentally kill me for poking fun?"

She gritted her teeth as she forced her magic back. "Let's cut to the chase, Mr. Draykon. I didn't kill that man. It would be stupid of me to do it in my own club where I'd bring attention to myself."

"Yes, it would be, but your friend here said it himself. Maybe the victim got you a bit churned up, and you lashed out. Maybe it was an accident."

Selena scoffed, but she said nothing while Shalik handed her a drink before placing one in front of the enforcer.

"Don't worry. It's just juice," he said as Draykon raised a questioning brow.

The enforcer gave him a nod of thanks before taking a sip of the drink. It was delicious, and he fought to keep the pleasant surprise off his face. Shalik smirked as though he knew what Draykon was trying to do.

"What about you, potion master? Did you kill the victim for trying to move in on your girl? Your territory?"

Shalik scoffed, his blue hair shaking as he shook his head. "Sorry to disappoint, but Selena is not my girlfriend. She's too high maintenance."

She shrugged as though she couldn't argue.

"And..." he went on. "Hacking someone to death is not my style. I like poison—quick, efficient and not so messy."

Draykon eyed the drink he'd been sipping. Again, the leather-clad man grinned. "You've got a sick sense of humor, do you know that?"

"Tell me about it," Selena muttered.

She locked eyes with him, silently communicating the pain of having to deal with a smart ass.

"Fine." Draykon gave her a small smile. His gaze shifted back and forth between them. "Do you know what the message on the steps means?"

Her hand jerked in Shalik's, and the potion master laid his palm over their linked ones. "No, she doesn't," he said in a tone that brooked no argument.

Draykon lean back in his chair. He knew they were lying, but he also knew if he pushed, they'd close ranks and he'd get nothing else from them, so he let it be for now. He stood, shoving his notebook and pen into his jacket pocket. "That's all the questions I have for you right now. When I have more, I'll have to meet you for another interview."

He stood and walked a few steps away, following the precisely cleared path through the glass.

"Enforcer Draykon?" Her soft but firm voice stopped him. "You never told me who the victim was."

He knew he hadn't. He'd wanted to see if she would ask. If she were the killer, she would already know. He turned back to the pair, his face neutral. "Huh, I thought I had." He pulled out the notebook as though consulting it. "I believe you have a restraining order against him. The victim's name is Lucien Mitchel, your ex-boyfriend."

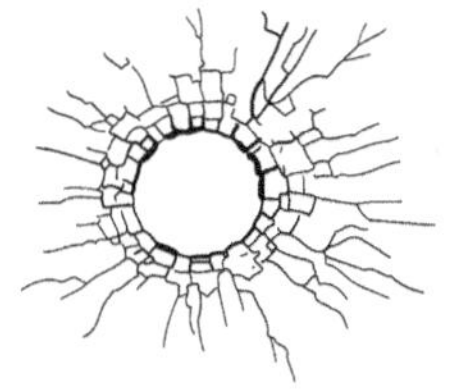

Chapter 8

Selena sat at her dining table, staring out through the wall-to-wall windows of her condo. Absently, she stirred the honey she'd added to her tea while the sunlight crept farther into the room. Soft snores and the occasional whining came from where Cerberus slept in his cage. She didn't notice, though. Just as she hadn't noticed her tea had gone cold a half-hour ago. The past consumed all her thoughts. Her mind reviewed every memory, every moment she'd had with Lucien. She'd loved him. Even when she sat in the dimly lit enforcer's office, signing the papers for the restraining order, she'd loved him. Selena had watched the ink dry on the document, and her heart had broken.

Maybe she'd loved him more than she should, but Lucien had been her first. The first being she'd given her heart and body to, and, in a way, her first wake-up call to the realities of this world. Back then, she knew he loved her. Well, he at least cared about her. But Lucien was a pixie. Translation—he could never rise to a higher power level because he wasn't a witch, human, or demon. He would forever stay on the lower rung of the power pole. It was why he became fascinated with her magic, why he'd pushed and prodded to see it at full strength, and why he loved it. Then she realized Lucien had grown to love her magic more than he'd loved her, and that was something she couldn't handle. So, she'd ended it.

But magic, for those who couldn't have it, was like a drug. It could twist them until their feelings became skewed. Lucien became obsessed with her, calling at all hours and begging to get back together. He would sit outside the old apartment she'd shared with Shalik and Mini, hoping to see her or "accidentally" run into her if she walked through the city or shopped with Mini. When Shalik and Mini had enough, they'd sat her down and convinced her that she needed to get a restraining order.

Selena started, the spoon clattering against the mug, as a shadow crossed her vision. Shalik squatted until they were eye level. His blue hair was tousled from sleep, his sweatpants hung low on his hips, and his feet were bare.

He gathered her hands in his. "How are you doing?"

She took a deep breath, then let it out slowly. "I'm fine."

He stared until she leaned forward, placing her head on his shoulder. "I can't get the image out of my mind, Li. I can't not see the body cut up and dead on the steps. His blood was every-where. That it was used to send me a message is horrifying."

He released her hands. Sitting on the floor he pulled her from the chair into his lap, he ran his hands up and down her back in a soothing manner.

"I can't believe he's gone, Li. I keep thinking that maybe he was in trouble, but he couldn't come to me because of the restraining order. This could be my fault." Her body shook as she spoke. "Maybe if I had given him more time, he could have changed. Learned to accept it the way you and Mini..."

"Shh," Shalik said, cutting off her what-if's. He continued to run his hand over her back while he spoke. "Don't think like that. This wasn't your fault. Lucien had his own issues, and he thought he could overcome them through you. You did the best thing you could for you both. Whoever did this to him is the one to blame. Not you. Nothing about this is your fault."

Her body gave one last shudder, then settled down. They stayed there for a while as Li held her, making circles on her back. They probably wouldn't have moved for even longer if someone hadn't knocked on her door. Selena climbed out of his lap and back into the chair while he stood and headed to answer it. She took a sip of her tea, grimacing at the cold liquid. Murmurs had her glancing over at the front door. She stood when Minerver walked in, an overnight bag in her hand. Their eyes locked. In an instant, all the bickering and fighting they'd been doing for the last few years melted away. In its place, the good times of their friendship took over. Selena crossed the distance between them, and Mini wrapped her up in an enormous hug.

"I tried calling," she said. "But when I didn't get an answer, I thought I would come over after the police had vacated."

"Okay." Selena's words were muffled in her friend's hair. Mini must have been in a rush if she hadn't taken the time to tame it. Then Selena's thoughts turned back to the night's events. "They killed him, Mini, to find out my secret, to find out more about my magic. At least he didn't know about my father..."

"Hush," Mini admonished. "We made a vow never to speak of it again. It's the best way to keep you hidden." She gripped Selena by the shoulders, leaning back to study her face. "If word gets out about your magic, Ofilia won't give you a moment's peace."

Selena sighed and pulled away. Walking back to the dining table, she plopped onto the chair she'd vacated. "I should have listened to you and taken the Hyōka. If I had, I would have been legally labeled a mid-level magic user, and Ofilia would have left me alone."

Miniver dropped her bag on the floor. She walked over to take a seat next to Selena while Shalik sat opposite them.

"Yes, but it would have been a risk, Lena," Shalik said. "One iota below or over the mid-point system, and you would be in the lower or upper caste. Either would have been a problem."

A mirror witch's power was rare. As a lower caste, she would have been forced to indenture like Shalik and Mini. Only in her case, the indentureship would be much longer as she could only indenture with high-powered masters who had to pay more for their servants. On the other hand, if she were a high-powered witch, the Council would force her to work for them and offer her "services" to the highest bidder.

"Yes, but then she'd be less open for scrutiny about her powers." Mini rubbed her temple. "You guys don't understand. Someone took pictures of everything outside the club. It's all over the news." She reached out to take each of their hands. "People are talking, Lena. They're speculating about your powers. The rumor is that you're a high-level mirror witch, and you've already come into your full powers." Mini let out a sigh. "It's only a matter of time before every low-level being is on your doorstep, asking for help. Or, worse, Ofilia starts auctioning off your talents."

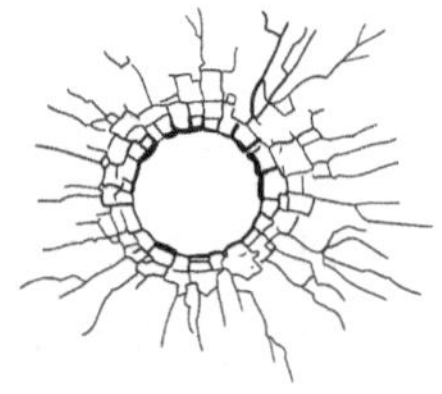

Chapter 9

Selena swore, her words colored with every emotion she felt. When she finished, Shalik raised a brow. "Feel better?" he asked.

"Yes, damn it." She laid her forehead on the table. "How can I fix this? I can't deal with everything *as well as* Ofilia and her hounds."

Miniver sighed as she was—in the public eye—one of Ofilia's hounds. "Take the stupid test."

Selena jerked upright. "What? We just said it was a bad idea."

"No... You and Shalik decided it was too risky. Years ago, I said you should have done it. Now, I'm saying it again. Do it. If you don't, everyone is going to speculate anyway. You need written proof that you're not a high-level mirror witch."

"But..." Shalik said.

"Look, I know things can go badly if she ends up at the wrong level," Mini said, her serious gaze moving to Shalik. "But it could be infinitely worse if Ofilia requests a summons, then forces Selena to take the test."

"She can't do that." Selena tightened her grip on Mini's hand.

"Yes, she can." Mini let out a sad huff. "You keep wanting to be ordinary, Lena, but you're not. Your magic is different—extraordinary—and so are you." Mini smiled. "I understand you're not ready to show the world who you are, and that's fine. Until you are, though, take the test. Otherwise, Ofilia is going to shut down the club. Remember, your new business license was issued on probation."

"What?" Shalik demanded. "Why didn't you tell me this?"

"I'm sorry," Selena snapped. "But someone dropping the dead body of my ex on my doorstep took precedence."

Mini held up her hand before they could start bickering. "Be that as it may, because your license is on probation, Ofilia has the right to shut down your business if she thinks you're not magically capable of protecting any citizen who visits your establishment. Not to mention," she went on, cutting the pair off when they opened their mouths to protest. "With a charge like that against a mirror witch, the only way to... prove your honor would be to take the test to show your level of magic is strong enough to protect them."

Selena rubbed her temples. "So, what you're saying is to take the Hyōka voluntary or else?"

Mini tapped her fingers on the dining table. "No. What I'm saying is to take control of the situation."

"Meaning?" Shalik asked, folding his arms over his wide chest.

"If Ofilia shuts you down and you're summoned to prove your magic is powerful enough, the test will be open. She already knows you lose control when you're angry, so she's going to find a way to provoke you to lose control. If she does, she'll get a more accurate reading on your magic."

"But if Selena volunteers to take it," Shalik said in excitement, "she could demand a closed-room test with whomever she wants as an assist."

"Fine," Selena said, tilting her head back to stare at the ceiling. "I'll do it. Just book a test as soon as possible... before that bitch gets any ideas."

Minerva grinned. "I'll make some calls."

She left them at the dining table and scooped up the handbag she'd dropped on the floor, fishing her phone out of the side pocket.

"Nice bag," Selena commented, noting the butter-yellow creation with the designer's name discreetly scrawled in red at the bottom left corner.

"Thanks," Mini murmured distractedly, scrolling through her phone for whatever number she needed. "I got it on sale along with a matching pair of shoes."

"Matching red sole?" Lena asked.

"You know it." Mini gave her a small smile before pressing the contact she'd been searching for.

Shalik scoffed. "You guys need to get past this merchandise obsession you have."

Selena glared. "I don't hear you complaining about merchandise obsession when you buy only organic products for your potions."

Shalik blushed. "Organic is healthy for you, and it makes the potions taste better and healthier."

"Ha, that's just a fancy way of saying you're a food snob."

"What?" Minever's screech had them turning their attention back to her.

"When did this happen?" she asked into the receiver. "But no notification was given to me. Why wasn't I told? An email?" she almost shouted. "I received no such thing. This is incompetence. When I find out who's responsible, there will be consequences." Mini ended her call, then squeezed the phone.

"You're gonna crush it if you keep doing that," Shalik commented.

"I take it you have bad news." Selena stretched out her legs, her feet barely touching the floor.

"I'm sorry, Selena," Mini said, her eyes closed in obvious frustration. "We're too late. Ofilia has already issued a summons for you to do the test."

Shalik's breath hitched. Selena's voice was resigned when she asked, "When?"

Mini opened her eyes, took a deep breath, and let it out in a whoosh. "Three days."

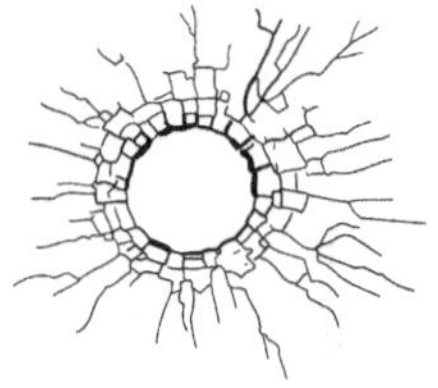

Chapter 10

Selena spent the three days she had overseeing the repair of her club. She had to have the glass replaced and the outside steps scrubbed and sanitized. Then, the glass had to be re-spelled so it once again told people their desires. She wondered if she should have bothered since she wasn't sure she could maintain her cool given the rage she felt against Ofilia. But it gave her something to do while Shalik worked on a soothing potion he felt could help keep her calm, and Mini tried to find a loophole in the system to have Selena tested in private. Mini's attempts had all been thwarted.

So today, Selena sat in the biggest public observation room in the Salva building. A split-level semi-circle of tile and white walls. The lower half was where she would perform the test requirements, while the upper part, walled off by protective glass, would seat the media and anyone who wished to observe her—if there were any spaces left.

In a matter of days, she'd lost her anonymity in Fusion City, and her life had been placed under a microscope. Everyone wanted her to possess the rare magic that brought equality to all magic wielders when the truth was everyone would be equal if they would only stop being little shits. If everyone treated others the way they wanted to be treated, all would be right with the world. Instead, they preferred to wait for someone to save them.

Well, tough.

Selena wasn't signing up for the job, and she wasn't going to sit on any pedestal or be anyone's sacrificial lamb. She came to Fusion City to enjoy her life, and she would not give that up to be the one true mirror witch. She glanced over at the Council, who, of course, had ringside seats on the lower floor. They too, had their own agenda for her powers, but they could suck it. She was no one's tool or weapon.

Selena took a deep breath, allowing the concoction Shalik had given her to calm her annoyance and frustration. She didn't glance up at the multitude of people on the upper floors, and she ignored the faint whispers that came through the glass as they observed her like a rat in a cage. Instead, she kept her eyes on Shalik, who was allowed to be there as her focus for the last part of the Hyōka.

The test was made up of three parts. The first was a standard cognitive check where she did math and wrote a short essay. Truthfully, she'd enjoyed writing about the Council, who was on a witch hunt and was wasting her time. Watching them read her thoughts had relaxed her even more. Then there was a medical checkup, made up of a vision test, blood pressure reading, and reflex check. The doctor who'd performed it had said she needed more vegetables in her diet. She'd given him the death glare he'd deserved while Shalik tried to hide his snicker. With the help of another of Ofilia's assistants—because she was so important that she needed a team of people—Mini was hooking up the wires to measure Selena's magic levels.

"Are you comfortable?" Mini asked, a slight frown between her brows.

"Yes," Selena answered. "But can I have a glass of water?"

"Here," Shalik said from behind Mini, anticipating Selena's needs. He held the glass to her lips, and she took a swallow.

"Thanks," she said. He gave her a brief nod, then placed the glass on the table near the tech tasked with observing her readings. In his late teens or early twenties, he was a young boy who probably had his hair styled at the same place Shalik did if the pink highlights in his afro were any indication. His skin was as dark as midnight, and he flashed his pearl white teeth as he chewed his bubble gum, blew a bubble, then popped. His head bobbed to what she assumed was music only he could hear from his wireless headphones. Selena watched in fascination as his fingers flew over the keys, pulling up whatever information he needed. After a beat, he turned to Minerver and gave her a nod. She and the other assistant stepped away, and she told Shalik he needed to take his seat. He took the opposite chair from Selena, and she focused her attention on him. He stuck his tongue out, and she smiled.

The tech cleared his throat, "Please begin," he said in almost a whisper.

With a slow inhale, she relaxed and allowed her power to flow through her, her skin glowing, the light refracting out from her. Shalik pulled out his shades, and Selena struggled not to laugh. She had to keep control of her magic; otherwise, the reading was going to blip up or down, and they'd be screwed.

Selena kept her gaze on Shalik's shaded face. She could still see his eyes behind the dark lenses, and she gave her power another push so the reading showed her abilities solidly in the middle range, then held it there. Shalik made an okay signal with his fingers, and she held her breath as the machines on the tech's table beeped and whirled. The tech's fingers once again flew over the keys of his machine.

"Hold..." the tech murmured

Sweat beaded on her brow as she fought to keep her magic from surging out. She could feel every reflective surface in the room. In her mind's eye, she could see the reflections of all the shocked faces. She gritted her teeth as the magic searched for a way to escape.

"Just a little longer..." the tech murmured again. Selena didn't know if he was naturally soft-spoken or if he'd been trained not to spook the test subjects, but if he continued to whisper, this test would be over soon because she was going to break every piece of power-rating equipment he used.

"It's okay, Lena," Shalik said, catching her attention. "You're almost done, then I have the perfect cocktail I'm going to mix for you. I'm calling it—*not the mirror witch.*"

Selena felt her power dip as she struggled not to laugh.

"Please don't lower your power until the test over," the tech murmured once again.

She wanted to smash his monitor. Abyss, she'd rather smash his face into it. Once again, she raised her power to mid-level, then breathed out her anger at the tech. Shalik gave her a small smile. He had purposely made her want to laugh so she could have a few seconds of reprieve. Now she was back under control, holding her magic at a steady level.

A minute later, the tech murmured, "You can drop your level now. The test is complete."

She closed her eyes, folding her power away.

"Well..." The grating voice had her eyes flashing open. Ofilia stood in front of her, dressed in her usual pale blue robes with a twisted smile. "That was underwhelming."

"Sorry to disappoint," Selena said, voice dripping with sarcasm.

"Personally, I thought it was quite entertaining," Raesean said, walking up to Ofilia's side. "Especially that lovely essay, but I don't think it warranted all this fuss for one..." He turned to the tech, raising a questioning brow.

"Mid-level six," the tech whispered even softer than before, his voice shaking slightly. One would think he was afraid of the demon Council representative. Nah, he couldn't be.

"Mid-level six," the demon repeated. "Now, if you'll excuse me, I have business to conduct, so I'll take my..." He winked at Selena. "What was it? Oh yes, my fine-suit-wearing ass to my other duties." She arched her brow at his reference to her essay, then shrugged in a, "I call 'em as I see 'em" manner. He gave her one last grin before walking away.

Miniver moved to unhook her from the machines, but Ofilia held her hand up. "I guess you have way less power than I thought. A shame you didn't have more. Maybe you could have protected your boyfriend from such a savage ending."

The machines began beeping and whirling, the tech's fingers once again flying over the keys of his machines. Selena's anger and magic surged higher. The lights in the room flickered, and the glass protecting the bystanders above began cracking. Screams echoed in the room, but Selena's focus was solely on Ofilia, who gave her a triumphant smile.

Then the tech shouted, leaping back from his machines as it sparked and smoke.

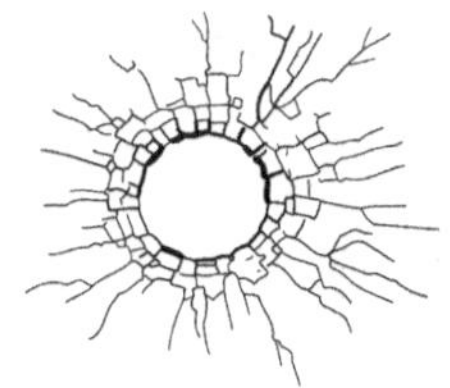

Chapter 11

"You did it, Lena." Selena grinned as Shalik popped another bottle of champagne, filling up the three champagne flutes he'd laid out on the club's bar. Valaria was in full swing, packed to capacity with well-wishers and others who were just ornery enough to want to see the spot where a dead body had been found. She shook her head. There were all kinds in this world.

Selena took the almost-overflowing glass from Shalik while Mini took the other. It was three days after her test, and she still couldn't believe they'd pulled it off. That bitch had provoked her into losing control of her magic. Worse, she'd made sure Selena was still hooked up to the Hyōka machine when she'd antagonized her. The machine had given Selena a new reading of six point eight before Mini had used her water magic to spill the glass of water Shalik had placed on the tech's table onto the machines. No matter how much magic there was, it was a universal law that water and technology did not mix. The result of the "accident" had started a mini fire, forcing another of Ofilia's assistant to rush in with a fire extinguisher. Any further chance of the tech getting things back online to run more tests had been ruined after that. Ofilia had been so furious that she'd said nothing more to Selena. Instead, she'd stormed out of the testing room. The memory made Selena's smile widen.

She clanked her glass against Shalik's and Mini's. "To the best friends a girl could have."

"To Lena," they shouted before they swallowed a mouthful of champagne. Selena turned to scan the crowd gathered on the dance floor, jammed in booths, or sitting around tables. Everyone was having the best time drinking potions that granted their wishes or just enjoying the alcohol. Selena had even sponsored a few rounds. Who cared that it set her back a few credits? It was only money. This carefree life was why she'd stayed in Fusion City, and now she could have it. With the Hyōka behind her and Ofilia off her case, she could finally let go.

"Dance with me," she shouted to her friends, placing the now-empty flute on the bar. Grabbing their hands, she pulled them out onto the floor. Music pulsed through her chest, the rhythm lighting up her blood, sending her body into smooth movements to match. She danced. Letting go of any inhibitions as she moved, magic glowing under her skin, escaping in her happiness. She danced with anyone who wanted to partner with her, switching from hand to hand, her body never pausing in its movements.

A fast Latin beat came on, and firm fingers grabbed hers. She didn't even hesitate, her body stepping into motion, her feet flying in time to the beat. Her partner moved her with grace and precision, his movements sure, guiding her where he wanted her to go. Selena was elated. In all her years of owning this club, she could count on one hand the number of times she'd found a great Latin dance partner. After a few minutes, the song ended, and Selena tilted her head back to get a better look at her partner. Her gaze traveled up a familiar body until she stared into the face of the demon's Council member. All her delight drained away.

She struggled, but he tightened his grip. "If I'd known you were such a brilliant dancer, Selena, I would have visited your club a long time ago." A small smirk played on his kissable lips. Selena felt her heart pick up a new beat that had nothing to do with dancing.

"What... How did you get in here?" she demanded, her voice sounding breathier than she liked.

He smiled, reaching up with one hand to coil one of her curls around his finger. "That rather interesting spell you put up only prevents beings with ill intent from entering your club. It doesn't stop demons."

"Then I ask again..." she said as she struggled to detangle her body and hair away from him. "How did you get in here?"

He slid the rest of his fingers into her hair, leaning down until his lips were a breath away from hers. "I'm not here to cause you pain—far from it. I want nothing more than to give you pleasure. Hours and hours of it if I could."

Fuck it.

She wrapped her fingers around the lapels of his suit. His eyes lit up in triumph. Then she brought her leg up, connecting solidly with the generous flesh between his thighs. His breath came out in a whoosh as he yanked his hand painfully out of her hair. The grip he had on her body loosened, and she took a step back.

Selena rubbed her scalp, sure he'd removed a few strands, but she couldn't help her smirk of satisfaction when he remained doubled over, hands on his thigh, panting.

"All you had to do was say no," he gritted out as he slowly straightened.

"The annoyance on my face should have been enough of a response," she huffed.

"I've seen you annoyed, Lena." He reached for her again, and she slapped his hand away. "And the face you gave me a minute ago wasn't annoyed."

"Is there some particular reason you're here sullying my club, Raesean?"

He opened his mouth. "Well..."

"Don't bother to answer that," she said, cutting him off. She turned on her three-inch heels and headed back to the bar. If she'd put an extra sway to her hips, it had nothing to do with the fact he was watching.

She slid onto a stool, and Shalik poured her a fresh glass of champagne.

"Are we gonna have a problem?" he asked, leaning closer to speak directly in her ear.

She shrugged. "That's what I'm waiting to see." She picked up her glass with one hand while the other played with the pendant on her necklace.

"You're such an ornery woman, yet you fascinate and draw me in." Raesean scooped the glass of champagne out of her hands and took a sip. He was smart enough to know he would never get service here, so he didn't bother trying.

"I don't care about your fascinations. I want to know what you're doing here—besides that, I want you to leave. You're killing the vibe in my club."

He looked at her, glass in hand, eyes going serious. "You pulled off quite the stunt the other day with Ofilia." He took another swallow of the drink.

"I don't know what you mean." Her face was the picture of innocence.

He arched a brow. "Right..." He placed the empty flute on the bar. "You and your friends need to be careful, Selena. It pissed Ofilia off that she couldn't trap you into being her cash cow with a higher reading."

"I don't give a shit about how pissed she was."

"You should be. I've known Ofilia for years. She holds a grudge, and she will be gunning for you and your friends."

"Is that a threat?" Selena slid to her feet.

He took a step away from her, looking out over the crowd of people who were trying their best to appear as though they weren't paying attention to what was going on by the bar.

"Like I said... I don't have any ill intentions toward you, Selena. I simply came to warn you." Saying nothing more, he turned and walked out of the club.

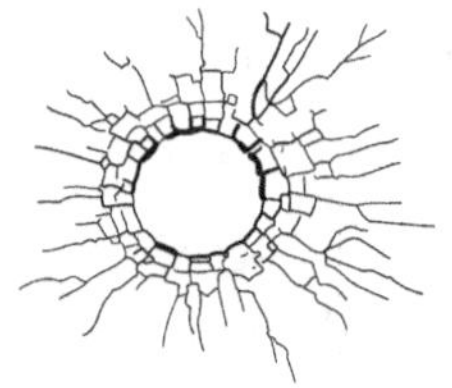

Chapter 12

Selena watched as Raesean left the club. His suit was impeccable, and his ass did his tailored pants justice. She let out a small sigh before turning back to the bar to brood into her empty glass.

"What's going on, Lena?"

Mini, who'd stayed a polite distance away from the conversation, shifted closer.

Selena shrugged. "Raesean thinks Ofilia is holding a grudge, and she's gonna find a way to get back at us."

"He's probably right." Mini mused. "The good news is that I can always keep an eye out on things for you."

Selena smiled. "So, you'll be my spy on Ofilia?"

Miniver drained her glass, then refilled it with the bottle Shalik had left on the countertop. He'd gone to the restroom somewhere between Raesean's stealing her drink and giving her a warning.

"Not spy per se," Mini continued. "I'll just be extra careful to review and copy any information on you in case we have to make a run for it."

"We?"

"Yes—*we*. Trust me, Selena, if Ofilia figures out we helped you, nothing will stop her from coming after us."

"True," Selena agreed.

"In that case, be prepared, Lena. If we have to run, we're going together."

Selena held out her hand. Mini grasped it and shook.

"Deal," they said in unison, then dissolved into fits of giggles.

It was something they'd done ever since they'd met in that filthy alley. Selena had been new to the city, not knowing the ins and outs, but it had captured her interest like nothing before. Miniver had lured some unsuspecting mark out the back entrance of a nightclub on the lower westside. She'd promised a series of sexual favors the human couldn't resist. What she'd actually planned was to have Shalik knock him out so they could rob him blind.

Selena stood in the shadows, the hood of her black robe pulled low. She watched in fascination as Mini drove the man's desires into a fever pitch. He was lost in the moment, forgetting where he was. He didn't see Shalik walking up behind him with a broken piece of wood, probably from a discarded crate in the same alley.

Maybe it was the way the man trembled in pleasure or the glint of the nail protruding from the wood in Shalik's hand, but Selena stepped forward. She wrapped her fingers around Shalik's wrist, staying his hand. He jumped, not expecting her to be there.

"Where the fuck did you come from?" Miniver demanded, pushing the man away. The mark, seeing them, deduced what was happening, turned, and scampered away.

Mini swore, then whirled on Selena, her eyes firing with anger. "You just cost us our payday, bitch."

"Better to lose the mark than to kill him." Selena took the piece of wood from Shalik, then turned it over so the nail showed.

Their eyes went huge. When Mini once again let loose a torrent of curses, it was for a different reason.

"I'm Selena, by the way," she said, tossing the wood a few feet away.

"Mini. This here," she said, hitching a thumb at the man next to her side, "is Shalik."

"I know," Selena responded. "I've seen you in different alleyways several times now—always relieving men of their valuables."

Mini cocked a hip. "Yeah. Well, everyone's got to eat."

"All right," Selena agreed. "How about teaching me to bring out people's desires? Maybe you can eat twice as much then."

Mini raised a brow, and Selena stuck out her hand to shake. "Deal?"

"Deal," Mini agreed.

They shared a smile at the memory. Mini swirled the contents of her glass, her eyes locked on Selena's. "You know, I never asked what you were doing in the alley that night. I mean... you just appeared out of nowhere."

Sighing, Selena slid her glass from left to right on the bar top. "I was there to work, and that's all I'll say about it."

"Okay, I..." Mini's voice trailed off as a wave of magic hit them, stealing their breaths.

Selena turned away from the bar, bringing her magic to the palms of her hands. She cast it out to trace the magical wave's source, using the mirrors in the club as a tracker. A thin line of light formed, leading out from Selena, past the half-drunk patrons, and straight to the club's restrooms. Selena and Mini rose, not hesitating to move past and ignore the intoxicated or enchanted patrons who could not sense the dark feel of the magical wave. The pair followed the glittering line into the unusually empty hall leading to the bathrooms. Selena's hands continued to glow as she kept her magic at the ready, and Miniver clutched her champagne flute. Not because she hadn't bothered to set it down, but because with her water magic, she could stuff the content in someone's nose and drown them. Death by champagne was not as pleasant as it sounded.

When they turned the corner, they almost stumbled over a body sprawled on the floor, blood pooling under his head.

"Shalik," Mini screamed, crouching to check his pulse. "He's breathing," she whispered, tears welling in her eyes.

Selena nodded, swallowing the lump of fear lodged in her throat. "Stay with him," she instructed.

"No," Mini said, struggling to her feet. "You can't go in there alone."

"Bloody Abyss, I can't. Stay with him, Mini. I don't want the person who did this coming back to finish what they started." Mini's gaze traveled between Shalik and Selena. "Stay, Mini. He needs you. I'll be fine. I'm all-powerful, remember?"

Mini gave her a watery smile before kneeling at Shalik's side. "Be careful, okay? I'm not far, so scream if you need me."

After agreeing, Selena took the last few steps to the men's bathroom, its door hanging askew on its hinges. Quietly, she stepped past the threshold into the dark room. The lights had gone out, leaving the room pitch black. She moved farther in, using the glow of her hands and the tracing cord to see. Her eyes darted in every direction, looking for movement, for anything to let her know if someone else was inside.

When her foot hit something, she stumbled back. Selena lowered her hands, casting her light toward the floor. Under the light of her magic, she saw the body of a man, with pale skin, laying spread eagle on the tiled floor. Carved into his chest, blood still seeping from the wounds, were four words.

I know your secret.

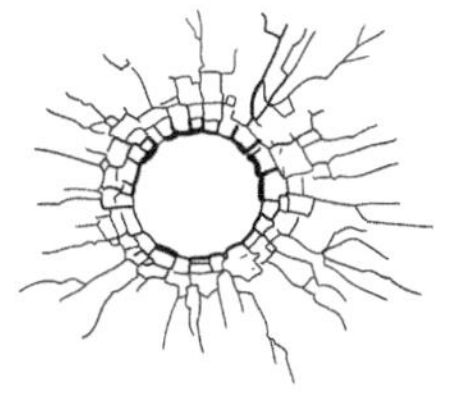

Chapter 13

Someone had turned on all the lights in Valaria, so it had lost its party atmosphere. Empty glasses, potion mugs, and vials littered abandoned cocktail tables and booths. The music no longer pumped through the speakers, making the empty club even eerier as the sounds of the enforcers and crime techs echoed while they worked.

Draykon stood off to the side, appearing amused as he gazed at the two women who flanked the potion master at one of the club's commandeered tables. A mystic examined the man, the pair watching her every move, ready to skin her alive if she caused him additional pain. The mystic took things in stride, mending the head wound, then checking him for any other injuries. Once finished, she left them to fuss over him.

"I'm fine," Shalik muttered, holding up his hands to keep them from crowding him.

That was the enforcer's cue to approach—not only to prevent the argument that was sure to follow but also to question them on what happened.

"Miss Decland, you seem to be racking up dead bodies in your club."

"Trust me, seeing you back here for another one is the last thing I wanted."

"I understand." He pulled out his notebook. "At least there doesn't seem to be a connection to you and this victim—a Mr. Harvey."

Selena swallowed. "Kent Harvey?"

Draykon eyed her. "Yes, judging by your expression, I guess my info was wrong."

She rubbed her eyes, smearing her makeup until it was less smoky and more raccoon. "I haven't spoken to Kent in years. He was a freelance bartender at a few clubs in the westside back when we..." She waved her hand at Shalik and Mini. "Used to live there. One day, he got a gig working for some high-level magical being and he disappeared. Haven't seen or heard from him since, and I haven't been back to the westside either."

"I see." Draykon made a note in his book. "Why don't you walk me through what happened tonight?"

They explained the night's events, including how Shalik went to the bathroom. Just before he left the facilities, he heard a noise. Before he could investigate, everything went blank. The next thing he knew, he was waking up in the hallway with Mini kneeling next to him.

"And you didn't see anyone or anything?"

Shalik shook his head, then winced. The two women practically pounced, looking him over to see where it could hurt. "I'm fine," he muttered. This time, though, he took Mini's hand.

Draykon raised a brow.

"Miss Pinkerton, why don't you take Mr. Sano somewhere he can get some rest? I'm sure the mystic advised he should after his ordeal."

Mini nodded, worry creasing her brow. After she helped the potion master to his feet, they slowly made their way to the upper part of the club, then to the elevator. For every step they took, Selena watched until they were out of sight. When they were gone, she turned hard eyes on him.

"Now tell me what you didn't want them to hear."

Draykon sat in one of the vacated chairs, pulled out a cigarette, and lit it.

"There's no smoking in here," she ground out.

He sighed, scanning for a place to put it out.

"Just finish the stupid thing." She pushed one of the empty cups that littered the table toward him to use as an ashtray. "You do know tobacco is from the Abyss, right? It's going to kill you."

He eyed her. "I hear congratulations are in order. Level six point eight. Cutting it close, aren't we?"

Her brows drew together, her face a mixture of confusion and suspicion. "What's that supposed to mean?"

He tapped his cigarette against the glass, ash dropping into the dregs at the bottom. "I heard the demon Council rep was here tonight."

"Are we about to play fifty questions? If so, I've got better things to do with my time."

Again, he eyed her. All that power packed into a five-feet-nothing package. He wondered when she would realize what he was. He shook his head to dislodge the thought. That subject was for another time.

"Enforcer Draykon, sir."

He glanced up at one of the crime scene investigators. "Yes, Tim?"

The man was young, probably not even past his twenties, and as fresh-faced as they came. His brain, however, was as equally big as he was innocent.

Tim cleared his throat. "The scene's ready for you."

"Thanks."

Tim stole a glance at Selena, who gave him a sultry smile. A blush crept over his features.

"Don't play with my team," Draykon muttered. Her eyes widened, the picture of innocence, but there was a mischievous sparkle in them.

"Go about your duties, Tim." The young man jolted, then scampered off. Draykon extinguished his cigarette in the cup, then stood. "Take a walk with me, Miss Decland."

She got to her feet, playing with her necklace. He jerked his head toward the bathroom where the body had been found, and she led the way.

"Have you decided to tell me what your secret is?" he asked from two steps behind her.

"I don't have secrets. If I did, it wouldn't be any of your business."

"It would be if someone out there is killing beings to get your attention."

"What others choose to do has no bearing on me."

"Just like your secret doesn't affect others?"

Selena stopped dead in her tracks, turned, and looked up "Do you have a point to make?"

"Just this. Whether you want to admit it or not, your secret is getting people killed. I have two bodies to prove it. Trying to hide it at this point is stupid," he said. "Secrets have a way of coming out. When they do, they always affect your nearest and dearest."

Fury sparked in her eyes. Without another word, she turned and stalked off, pushing open the bathroom door. They had removed the body, and the lights had been restored. She stepped forward, her heels clacking against the tile with each slow step. Her eyes locked onto the blood markings forming a perfect circle where the body had lain. She stopped a few inches away and crouched, stretching her hands over it.

"These symbols," she whispered.

"Yes." He waited for her to continue.

"It's the old language of the demons, a ritualistic language. It was used to make a demon circle to sacrifice people to Abaddon in the Abyss before he put a stop to it."

"Yes."

She gazed up "Only the older demons would know about these."

"I know," Draykon said, reaching for his pack of cigarettes before he remembered where he was.

She stood, straightening to her full height. "That's why you asked me about him?" She stared into his eyes, dread showing in hers. "You think the demon Council member is the one committing the murders, and Abaddon's minion knows my secret?"

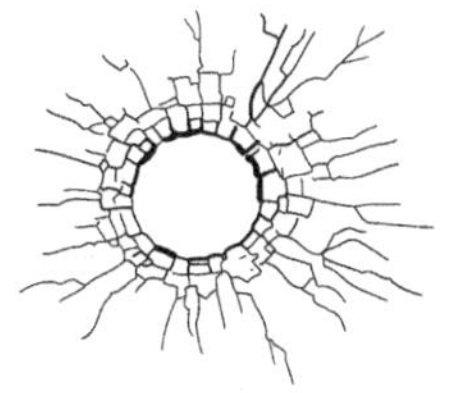

Chapter 14

Selena's heels had barely hit the sidewalk when the taxi driver pulled off. The back door of the cab slammed close in his haste. She couldn't blame him. He'd dropped her off on the lower westside of Fusion City, demon territory—affectionately termed Debauchery City or DC. Selena hadn't been back here since she, Mini, and Shalik had lifted enough money from their marks to move out of DC into a shitty apartment on the lower eastside.

She stood on the sidewalk in front of Club Bacchus. Dressed in a pale gray micro-mini dress, she was about to confront the demon Council member in his own nightclub. Worse, she'd chosen to come alone. Something that had turned the heated discussion she'd had with her friends about the demon's involvement into a full-blown shouting match. Shalik had wanted to come, but he was still recuperating. Mini couldn't because if they were wrong about the demon, she could lose her job, and there was no way in the Abyss she was taking the enforcer as Shalik had suggested. One look at him, and they wouldn't get past the club doors. Everyone knew the club was known for being lenient with all illegal activities. They would never let her in with him, and Selena would never get the answers she needed. No, she had to do this alone. If she felt a tiny bit of anticipation in seeing Raesean again, then so be it.

Selena carefully picked her way over the uneven sidewalk. Her dress clung to her every curve, ending a few inches below the cleft of her ass. If she shifted wrong, she'd be flashing more than her legs. She took a shallow breath as the stench from a nearby alley assaulted her, causing her eyes to tear up. The faint squeaks of rodents could be heard as they scurried about. Stifling a shudder, she put on an alluring smile and faced the bouncer in front of the club. As with all Raesean's employees, he was dressed in a suit and appeared as if he took no shit from anyone.

"One, please," she said. Her voice came out sultry, filled with the promise of intimate moments.

The guy folded his tree-trunk-sized arms over his wide chest, the material of his jacket straining. The club's lights bounced off his bald head, and he narrowed his black eyes No iris or pupils—just an unending dark, a sign he was mixed with troll. "Private party tonight," he rumbled.

Selena didn't miss a beat. "Yes, I know. I was invited, and I don't have a plus one so... it's only me here for the party."

"Invitation," he demanded.

Selena huffed. "Obviously, I didn't walk with it," she said, gesturing to her body and the small clutch she'd brought along.

The man shifted his stance as though digging in his heels. "No invitation, no entry."

Selena was about to tell him exactly what she thought about that when a familiar voice drifted from the doorway of the club. "Let her in, Sig."

Selena smiled in triumph.

The man, Sig, turned and frowned at the man in the doorway. "But the boss said no invitation, no entry."

The spiky dark-haired demon, dressed in a stellar suit, shook his head with a small smile. "Trust me, the punishment would be worse if you don't let this one in. She's one of the bosses... preferred girls."

Selena bristled at the term, but she held her tongue. She needed to get inside. If Sig let her in because he thought she was a hooker, so be it. He perused the length of her body, and she fought the urge to deck him. But he finally shrugged, then stepped aside. She moved quickly, climbing the steps to the door until she was face to face with the demon.

"Alden," she said with a smile, kissing both his cheeks. "It's been too many years."

"It most certainly has." When he offered his arm, she hooked hers through it. He led her at a leisurely pace down the hall to the open floor of the club. "I believe the last time I saw you, you were half drunk and screaming good riddance to DC."

Selena laughed. "That would have been the night before the four of us moved into the apartment on the lower eastside."

"Ah yes, the quartet. You guys were inseparable and insufferable."

Selena bumped her hips against Alden's. "Oh, come on. We were young then, dreaming of the high life and bigger and better things."

"And you got bigger and better. Granting people's desires and forgetting us poor peons down on the lower westside."

"Please," she said, waving dismissively. "As Raesean's right-hand man and a top-ranking officer in Abaddon's army, you're hardly a peon."

He grinned. "Well, serving in the Abyss has its perks."

"As does granting people's desires."

Alden barked out a laugh, patting her on the arm. "You do have a point, lovey. So, what brings you slumming to this part of town, Selena?"

She grinned. "I'm here to see your boss, actually."

He stopped in his tracks, halting her forward movement. "Why?"

"Don't worry... I'm not here to make a deal with him."

Alden let out a breath. "Okay. You do know it's never a good idea to make a deal with a demon, right? There's always a catch, or they double-cross you."

Smiling, Selena shook her head. "Still looking out for me, Alden, after all these years."

He sighed. "I'll always have your back, Selena. You know that." He gave her a small smile. "Even though you threw me over for the pixie. So, what happened to him?"

The smiled she'd had died. "He's dead."

"I... I... I'm sorry, Lena. I didn't know. I-I would never..." Alden stammered.

"Forget it," she said, unlinking her arm from his. He grabbed her before she could completely pull away.

"Really. I'm sorry, Lena. I know how much you cared about him. If I can do anything, let me know."

Selena sighed. "It's fine. Just take me to your boss."

Alden nodded, walking them forward once again. "All right, but talking to him at this party might be a little difficult."

She frowned. "What do you mean?"

"The party is ah..." He parted the heavy silver drapes that blocked the view to the club's main floor. "Well, see for yourself."

She moved into the open area, then stopped dead in her tracks.

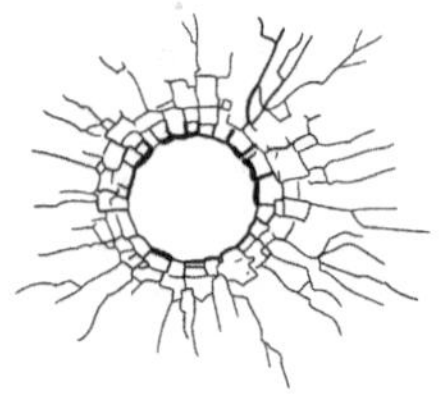

Chapter 15

Bodies in various stages of undress filled the converted dance floor. Selena's eyes widened as she watched beings in pairs, threesomes, quartets, and more touch and be touched in the public setting. Some engaged in their activities on lounge sets or thick rugs, while others balanced against the walls. Frozen, she gaped at the scene. She couldn't help but look, even though she didn't want to. Entwined arms, legs, and bodies moved to the rhythm of the seductive music pumping out of the speakers. Selena could feel herself blush and was glad no one was paying her any attention.

Someone touched her shoulders, and she jumped. Alden chuckled. "I'd think someone of your jaded nature, who grants people's desires, would have seen an orgy party before."

Huffing, she took a step away from Alden. "I help people get magical desires, not basic ones. Even if I did, I certainly wouldn't put them on display like this."

A woman screamed her pleasured release, and Selena's gaze darted back to the scene. Alden laughed. "You might pretend to be a prude, Lena, but I know you." He ran a delicate finger over her exposed arm. "You're as hot-blooded as they come. Don't think I don't know that watching this group pushes *all* your buttons."

"Am I interrupting?" The deep voice that cruised over her skin did more to jump-start her engines than the entire scene in front of her. Selena looked up at Raesean, who was ironically dressed in a suit the same color as her dress. He'd slicked his snow-white hair into a short tail, and he wore a matching mask that highlighted his blue eyes. The blue was so pale it was almost white, although his eyes held a sharp edge as he gazed directly at Alden.

"No, you're not interrupting," she blurted. The last thing she needed was a pissing contest between these two.

Alden smiled, shifting away from Selena before he stuck his hands in the pockets of his dark slacks. "Catch you later, Lena," he said, turning and heading back down the hall.

Raesean's eyes landed on her, taking in every part of her exposed body. A slow smile crept over his lips, and Selena's mind went blank for a couple of beats.

"Have you come to be the hostess to my host for this soiree?"

Selena stole a quick glance down at her fingers, which were running double-time over the clutch in her hands in a pitiful attempt to gather her wits. She lifted her head to meet his eyes. "No, I needed to speak with you in private."

"I would be more than happy to talk to you in... *private*." The last sounded decadent, inferring the conversation would be far more intimate than just words.

"Cut the crap, Raesean. I'm not here to play games. I need answers." When she scowled, he arched a brow.

"All right." He held out a hand. "We can talk in my office."

She glared at his hand as though it would bite, and he laughed. "Don't worry. I'm not going to try anything, even though we both know it wouldn't take much to distract you. You wanted to talk, and my office is on the other side of this room." He pointed to the glass room that was a floor up from the people copulating in plain view. "I don't want you getting lost among the guests. They tend to frown upon being magically abused at an invitation only party."

With another glance into his eyes, she placed her hand in his.

His eyes widened a little like he hadn't expected her to give in, but he wrapped his long fingers around her tiny ones. It was like a dance, but not the hot, pulsing movements they shared before on the dance floor. No, this was alluring. He moved her with skill through the gathering. Shifting her to his side when a hand reached out, turning her away when someone stepped in their path, lifting her over splayed legs and hands until they were at the stairs leading to his office. Her shoes clicked with each step up the stairs. She could feel his eyes roving over her body as he followed behind. "If you don't stop staring, people are going to get the wrong idea about where we're going."

His chuckle was dark. "Trust me. If anyone here is thinking about us at the moment, it's not in a platonic way."

Selena stumbled as she hit the landing, and he chuckled even more. He stopped on the step just before the landing and pulled her close to whisper in her ear. "You like that idea? Someone thinking about you while in the throes of passion? If that's the case, then I have a plethora of fantasies I can give you."

She jerked away, her heart racing, but she refused to let him know how much he affected her. "No one wants to hear about your sick fantasies while you're banging the hooker of the hour, Raesean."

"Who said I had company while I was thinking of you?"

Her jaw dropped as a variety of thoughts assailed her. "I..."

"Don't bother denying it." He interrupted. "You like knowing I'm thinking of you in the filthiest of ways. But like you said, you didn't come here for those reasons. Come." Grasping her hand, he walked her down the short hall to the office. He placed his hand on the embedded palm scanner, and the door unsealed with a whoosh. He motioned for her to walk in first.

The room wasn't as elaborate as she thought it would be, especially for a demon of his stature. There was a functional desk with a lamp and papers strewn over it. One visitor's chair sat in the front with an executive chair behind the desk. A floor-to-ceiling bookshelf was off to the far right, filled with various ledgers. The most comfortable-looking item in the room was the sofa on the left. Selena ventured farther inside, her heels whispering over the plush carpet.

"This is not what I expected," she said. She turned to look out the glass window only to get an aerial view of the party downstairs. She about-faced quickly, refusing to look at Raesean, then headed to the sofa and lowered herself into the far corner. He watched her the same way a lion would a gazelle after a two-month fast. When she cleared her throat, he shifted his gaze from her legs to her eyes.

"Did you kill that man and leave him in the bathroom of my club?"

"What?" he demanded.

Selena let out the breath she didn't know she'd been holding. For whatever reason, she didn't want to acknowledge she hadn't wanted it to be him. By his shocked expression, it wasn't him unless he was a better actor than she thought. If that were the case, he should cut a deal with the humans to make movies. He'd make a fortune.

"Why would you think I would murder someone and leave them in your bathroom?"

"Why were you at my club?"

"I already told you why—I was there to warn you." He removed his mask then ran a hand through his hair, loosening the tie that held it back. Loose strands fell forward to frame the sharp edges of his face, and her fingers itched to push them back. "Ofilia has the biggest hard-on for you. That's saying something, considering..."

"Considering what?"

"Considering she's a woman." He grinned, the shock of her question wearing off.

Selena smirked. "Women can get hard-ons, too. It's called lady wood. But..." She held up a hand to stop the remark she knew was coming. "I don't think her desire for power would make her murder two people and leave them on my doorstep."

"If she knew your secret, she might." He walked closer, then took a seat on the other end of the sofa.

She glanced away. "I don't know what you're talking about."

"Oh, please, Selena. I know you're a high-level mirror witch. I've known ever since you arrived in Fusion City and started picking up marks in my club."

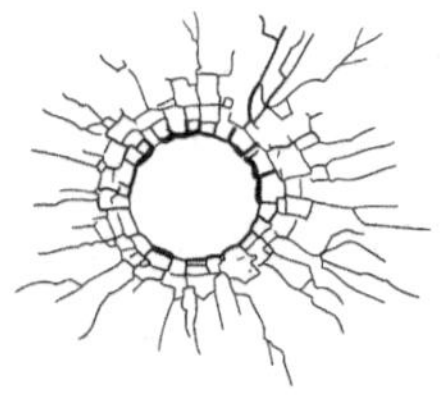

Chapter 16

Selena laughed. "I don't know what you're talking about."

A look was enough to convey his disbelief.

"Fine," she conceded. "I have a large quantity of mirror witch powers, but I can't transfer magic to others despite what everyone thinks."

"But you can eventually. If the prophecy and stories are true, then as a high-level mirror witch, that power can eventually be reincarnated in you."

"That power won't come to me," she insisted. Her fingers tightened on her clutch, her eyes locking unto his.

He held her gaze, expression saying he knew there was more to the story, but he didn't ask.

Selena averted her eyes. "Anyway, I never understood why you didn't stop us from picking up marks in your club. We must have been bad for business."

He shrugged. "This is DC. If you leave here only having lost a few credits and your dignity, then you should be glad.

Besides, you guys were always sure to leave the marks in one piece, especially when you started using your mirror trick to mesmerize them instead of Mini's wood-to-the-head method."

She arched a brow. "How did you know I used my magic?"

"Are you kidding me?" He grinned.

Selena felt like she was missing something, but she didn't know what.

He shook his head. "The men you guys robbed always came back to the club looking for you."

"What?"

"Yes. When they first came to, they would talk about seeing a bright light and having the most fantastic dreams where all their desires came true. My men would laugh and offer them congratulations, as they'd just been mirrored. Then my men would send the marks on their way. The strange thing was that even though they lost every cent to you and your crew, they came back. Sometimes days or weeks later, but they would always come back in search of you, wanting to be mirrored again."

Selena sat stunned.

"Didn't you noticed that your marks were a bit familiar, and they started getting easier and easier to get after a while?" He laughed.

Selena scrunched her forehead in thought. "Some of the men no longer had wallets on them, only a few hundred credits."

"That's because they knew the deal."

"What deal?"

"When you showed up, we would give them a call. They came to the club, paid a fee, Alden would 'accidentally' let it drop who was spending that night, and then you and your crew would relieve the mark of his payment. The club got a cut, you got your credits, and the mark got his fix. Everyone won."

"Son of a bitch."

He chuckled. "Oh, come on. I couldn't very well have you making money in my club without a fee. What kind of demon do you take me for?"

"One with scruples," she grumbled.

"No such thing, sugar." He leaned over and pulled on a tight curl, watching with fascination as it bounced back into place. "I could have made a deal with you, but I doubt you would have accepted. Back then, you were even more wary of demons than you are now. Much to Alden's disappointment."

Selena eyed him as he reclined into his corner of the sofa.

"Tell me why you think I murdered that man." It was as though the thought of Alden brought the demon back to the reason she was there.

"There were demon markings under the body."

"How do you know it was demon markings?"

"I just know."

He frowned. "You're a conundrum, Selena." When she said nothing, he went on. "The language of the demons hasn't been used on the surface world for decades. It's sometimes used in the Abyss, but only the older demons have any idea how to."

"You're not telling me anything new here, Raesean. It's why I suspected you." she drummed her fingers on her thigh.

"I see. Not that you would believe me, but it wasn't me. If I wanted to send you a message, I would send you a note and some flowers. Wooing women with dead bodies is too 18th century for my tastes."

A giggle escaped Selena before she could stop it.

"I never thought I would hear that sound coming from you because of me." He looked almost sad.

She smoothed away imaginary wrinkles in her dress. "Don't get used to it."

"I know, your tough reputation would crumble if anyone knew you giggled."

"Exactly."

"Well, then." He let out a breath. "I could look into any demons who might be old enough to know the language. Maybe one has discovered your secret."

Selena narrowed her eyes. "And what would I have to do to get this information?"

"Spend a night with me."

"Forget it." She pushed off the sofa and got to her feet, shoving her clutch under her arm as she started for the door.

"No. Not like that," he rushed out. "A night out, just the two of us, on a date." He was rambling, an oddity for him.

Selena stopped. "A date?"

"Yes. You know, something that two beings interested in each other do."

"I know what a date is." She shifted from foot to foot. "That's it? A date?"

"Yes. Just one night out."

She frowned. "Why?"

"My reasons are my own. If you want the information, then agree."

"Okay."

"Okay, as in yes, you agree to the deal?"

If Selena didn't know better, she would have said he sounded shocked. "Yes, I agree to the deal as long as I'm returned home unharmed and no sex is involved."

He stood, buttoning his suit jacket, his smile a mile wide. When he held out a hand, she grasped it and shook. "Congrats, Selena. You've just made your first deal with a demon."

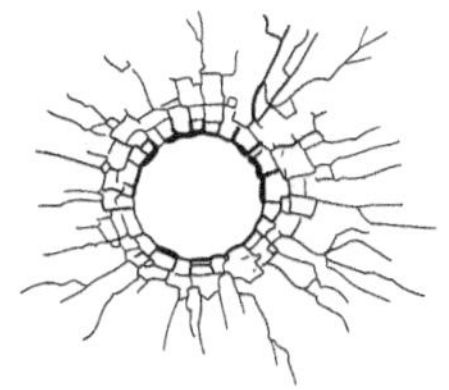

Chapter 17

Raesean stood on the club steps, watching as Selena climbed into his town car. He'd called it around for her, though she'd tried to decline his "no strings attached" offer. She eventually caved when he'd explained that she might have been able to trick the taxi into bringing her to DC, but there was no way she could get one to come back to pick her up.

Now she settled herself in the backseat and glanced up at where he stood on the upper tier of the steps. A heartbeat later, the sleek black car pulled off. Minutes ticked by, but he remained standing there, one hand in his pocket and feeling like a complete fool. He wasn't one hundred percent sure why he'd done it—why he'd pushed that deal with her. What he knew for sure was that from the moment he'd laid eyes on Selena De-cland, she'd sparked a warmth in him that not even the hottest flame he could magically generate would heat. He'd spotted her in his club, sitting with the water witch and the potion master, although back then, no one knew for sure what his powers were.

The woman was dressed in black skinny jeans and a slinky red blouse. Her taller friends almost overshadowed her short stature, but she still shone. No one could take their eyes off her, yet she sat—oblivious to the stares—eyes riveted on everything in his club, sipping on a pink cocktail.

He watched her for most of the night before his curiosity had finally drawn him to her.

"Minerver, Shalik," he said, acknowledging the pair before turning his eyes back to her. "I've lived in DC for many years, but I've never seen you before."

"Selena," she said, unwrapping her fingers from around her drink to give him a small wave. "I'm not from DC."

"Where are you from, Selena?" Her sultry voice only increased his curiosity.

"Here and there," she said evasively.

He arched a brow. "And how long are you planning to stay in Fusion City?"

She smiled. "I've decided on an extended stay."

"I see." He couldn't help but returned her smile.

"So, Mr...."

"Raesean, just Raesean."

"So, Raesean, what do you do?"

"This and that," he teased in return.

"Raesean owns the club," Minerver cut in.

Selena frowned. "I thought you guys said a demon owned the club."

"I am," he confirmed. He watched as any warmth she'd previously offered turned to a chill so sharp it could have been blade used to cut a line between them.

"Well then," he said. "Enjoy your night."

Later, he'd learned that she was just as cold with any demon she came into contact with, though she never failed to fascinate them, especially Alden, who was the only one who'd come close to thawing that icy regard of hers, a fact that still fanned the flames of Raesean's jealousy. He supposed that as time passed, he'd pressed his luck with her, provoking her anger so he could get some other reaction from her other than the cold resilience, never believing that anything would come of it. Until he'd read her essay, a masterpiece that blatantly described how she felt about the Council, the system used to indenture lower beings. He'd read what he knew was obviously a slip in her anger when she'd written that *he could take his fine-suit-wearing ass back to the Abyss and take Ofilia with him.* He'd grinned when he read it, but it also let him know she wasn't oblivious to his charms. So, when she'd come to him, when he'd seen a way to get closer to her, he took it.

Raesean shook himself hard before he turned and headed down the hallway to the evening's activities. A scenario that completely bored him, but business was business and he had to keep up appearances. Alden unfolded himself from the shadows in the hall to stand at his side.

"So, what brought the princess of mirrors down to the west-side this time of night? Has she finally began warming up to you?"

Raesean turned to his right-hand man. Alden was only in the position because of his loyal service to Abaddon. He suspected that Abaddon had appointed Alden the post to monitor him. He also suspected that Alden also delivered his own reports to Abaddon about Raesean's deals and since he didn't want Selena on his master's radar, he answered his right-hand man rather than reprimand him for asking questions that were none of his business.

"She came to accuse me of being a murdering bastard. I've management to convince her I'm not. Thus, I'm free to return to my duties."

As though realizing he'd over stepped his bounds Alden bowed and folded his shadow over himself, disappearing into the darkness.

Raesean returned to the party, splitting his mind between being host and what Selena had told him. There was a rogue demon using the old language to send her a message. As sure as the hellfire in his veins, he knew that if a demon was fixated on her, they wanted something. Something that only she could give them, and they would stop at nothing to get it from her, even if they had to carve it from her corpse.

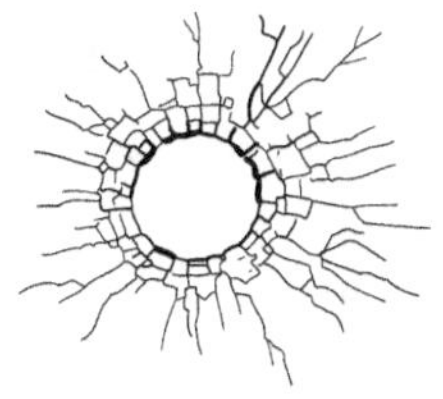

Chapter 18

Selena stood with a cup of tea in her hands, staring out the windows of her apartment. She took a sip as she watched the city bustling below. She could almost hear the blare of car horns, the angry shouts of taxi drivers, and the busy movements of beings as they hurried to their destination. All the activity of the city paled in comparison to the different thoughts running through her mind. Though one particular thought kept popping back in unwanted.

Why, of all the things Raesean could ask for, would he ask for a date?

Demons were notorious for being selfish, seeking their own pleasure above all. It was the reason people were wary of making deals with them. They always had a hidden agenda or would double-cross anyone, especially if qualifiers weren't added to the deal. But Raesean didn't so much as blink when she added hers, and she couldn't see any reason he would want a date with her. Sex, yes—what male didn't want sex? Him wanting a date, though, confused her. To add to the confusion was the way he told her he profited from her history of thieving. Why hadn't he tried to cut a deal with her then? He'd had all the means to corner her into making one. Why hadn't he pressed his advantage?

Selena sighed.

"Still no word from the demon?" Shalik padded up to her side by the window to look down at the city.

"Nothing. It's been a week. You would think he would have *some* news." Taking a sip of tea, she watched as a bright green taxi ran straight into the back of a sports car. She winced. "Someone's care car rights payment just went up."

"Or an indentured worker just added more years to his sentence," Shalik mumbled.

Selena sighed again, this time for a different reason. "In a few years, you'll be free, then we can start the scholarship fund we talked about. Work with other freed indentures to help others."

"I suppose," he mumbled again, this time turning away from the view and heading into the kitchen.

"What do you mean? I thought that's what you wanted?" She followed him, then took a seat at the dining table.

"Yes, I do, but with all that's been happening, I feel like you've changed your mind."

"What? That's absurd," she scoffed, running her hands over the warm mug.

"Is it?" He reached into the fridge, then began pulling out the ingredients to make an omelet.

"Yes, it is. I've never deviated from my plans to help inden-tures. It's not my fault someone is dropping dead bodies on our doorstep."

"I never said that it was."

"Then what are you saying, Shalik, because you sure as shit aren't making sense?"

He slammed the frying pan on top of the stove, and Selena jumped. Then, hands on his waist, he bent over, his breaths coming in short pants as though he were fighting to suck in air.

Selena hurried over to him. "Hey, what's wrong?"

She rubbed his back, making slow circles between his shoulder blades. After a few moments, he stood and wrapped his arms around her. When she buried her face in his chest, he laid a cheek on her head. "You know when that person attacked me, the last thought I had before I blacked out was that they were going to kill you and Mini next. That I was dead, and they were going to get you both. I've never felt so helpless, Lena."

"It's okay. It's okay," she whispered. "Don't worry about what might have been. Let's work on what we know and try to catch the bastard."

"That's just it, Lena. We don't know anything. We don't know what their agenda is, and this person could kill us at any time."

"I don't believe they want us dead. Otherwise, why go through all this trouble? No, they want something from me. I just need to figure out what it is."

Shalik took another breath as he held her at arms' length. "Okay but I have question."

She smiled. "Shoot."

"What's going on with you and Raesean?" He held her firm as she tried to wiggle out of his grip. "I know you've had the hots for him since we lived in DC, so tell me the truth. What's going on?"

"Nothing," she huffed. He arched a brow.

"Okay, Mr. Nosy. What's happening between you and Mini?" She looked at him expectedly.

"We hooked up, and we're taking things slow."

Her jaw dropped open in shock. "Really!" Selena let out a squeal high enough to break every glass she had in the apartment.

"No," he said, and she pouted. "But we've been talking about us. How we've always felt about each other."

"Finally." She pumped a triumphant fist in the air.

"Yeah, I think me getting hit the head was a wakeup call for both of us." He gave her a rueful smile.

She bounced up and down as much as Shalik's grip would allow. "We should celebrate, maybe a party."

"No. No parties until the enforcers have determined how the body got into the club. Or at least until the demon can give us some insight into this."

"Aww."

"No. You know it's too dangerous. We don't need to give Ofilia a reason to pull the club's license. We're already on shaky ground with her as it is."

"Fine, but one day, that bitch is going to get what's coming to her. I swear."

"Yes, but in the meantime, let's not have her close the club before we do."

"Okay. So, what are we going to do for business if we can't open the club?"

"I have an idea, so let me worry about that."

Selena shrugged. "You're the brains behind this operation. I'm just the name."

"You're more than that. You're smart—smart enough to try to change the subject until I almost forgot I asked you a question."

"It was worth a shot." This time when she pulled, he released her, knowing she needed to pace in order to tell him her story.

"Nothing has happened between us. Yet," she added when he raised a brow.

"But you're torn about it."

"Yes. I mean, even though he's sex on a stick and I just want to take big, juicy bites."

Shalik held up a hand. "I get the picture."

"You asked," she said with a shrug. "I'm still wary of him."

He ignored the comment. "He's also the first guy you've been into since Lucien."

She walked over to the dining table and sat. "Yes, he is."

Shalik joined her at the table. "He's dangerous, Lena. If you get involved and he finds out who you are, who your father is…"

She stood, pacing once more. "Don't you think I know that? I've learned that lesson the hard way, with Lucien, and he wasn't even a demon. He just wanted to not be indentured."

"Lena," he murmured.

"No, don't bother patronizing me. I know who I am, who my parents are. I've had to hide the truth just to have a normal life. Trust me, it sucks. It sucks that people I care about are in danger because I'm in hiding, and it sucks that everyone wants a piece of me only because of the power they think I can give them." She wiped at the tears now streaming down her face. Shalik stood and gathered her to him.

"It's gonna be okay."

"No, it's not, Li. If we don't find this person soon, we'll lose everything. The club, your indentureship, everything… and I'll have to leave."

"No, don't say that."

"You know it, I know it, and I bet Mini knows it, too. If we don't find the person who's doing this soon, the only other way to stop them and protect everyone is for me to go back home. To the Abyss."

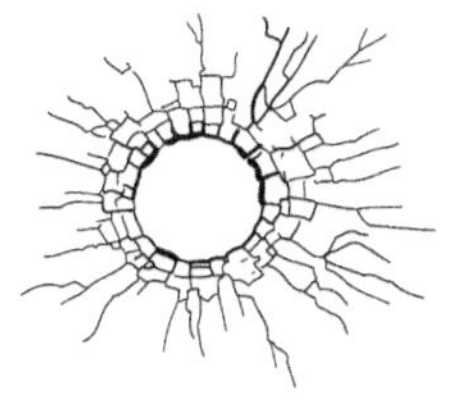

Chapter 19

Shalik said nothing. There was nothing to say because she'd only said the truth. Instead, they stood there for a while, clinging to each other. Lost in thought. The shrill tone of her cell caused them to separate. Selena scrubbed a hand over her face, then walked over to the center table in the living room where she'd left it. She smiled at the display name.

"Hey, Mini," she answered before plopping onto the sofa.

"Hey yourself." Her voice was soft, almost like a whisper.

"Is something wrong?"

"No, No... I-I just saw something weird. Something that might explain who knows about you."

Selena straightened on the sofa. "What did you find?"

"I can't say right now. I'll tell you more when I stop by tonight. I have to head over to Ofilia's first to drop off some documents she needed to review before tomorrow, but I'll be by right after."

"All right..." Selena said, drawing out the words in her worry.

"Have you heard from the demon?" Mini whispered.

"No, I haven't. Mini, what's going on? Are you okay?"

"Yes, I'm fine. Just ask the demon about the pit, okay?"

"Okay."

"Gotta go."

"Be careful, Mini. Remember our deal. If anything goes down, we run together."

"I remember. Love you both. Bye, Lena."

The sudden silence told Selena that Mini had hung up. Selena replaced the phone on the center table before flopping back on the sofa. Shalik peered over the side.

"What's going on?" His eyebrows were drawn together.

"Mini said she found something," she mumbled, her mind churning, wondering what it could be and what pit she was talking about.

"What did she find?" he asked

"She said she'll tell us later when she drops by, and to ask Raesean about a pit."

"You gonna call him?"

"Maybe later. I want to see what Mini found first in case I have to make another deal to get the information."

Shalik's lips thinned. Selena rolled her eyes.

"We've been over this. I had to make the deal. It's just one date, and I added qualifiers."

"I just don't understand why he had to make a deal and why you took it."

"You know demons don't do anything without some benefit for them. It's not in their nature."

"But..."

"No buts. That he hasn't asked for more is what's concerning me. I mean, he sort of knows my secret, and he hasn't asked for anything pertaining to that."

Shalik folded his arms over his chest. "That's the other thing—how do we know it's not him sending you dead bodies to get your attention?"

Selena snorted as Raesean's words about wooing women came back to her. "It's not his style. But I'm going to wait until we get some concrete evidence before we accuse a Council member."

"Very well," Shalik agreed.

"Now, are you gonna make breakfast or you just gonna let me starve?"

"Fine, but I'm putting spinach in the omelets."

"Oh, come on," she said with an exaggerated whine. She was rewarded with a small chuckle.

While Shalik beat eggs for the omelet, her mind went back to Mini. Though she'd said she was okay, Selena couldn't help the worry eating at her stomach.

* * *

The dream was like any other. Events taking place with no beginning, no sign how she got there. The room was circular with smooth walls, as though she stood in a vertical concrete tube. It was washed in a dull red light so that everything looked as though it was covered in blood. Shadowed figures moved around the room, chains rattled against the floor, the metal pinging off the concrete.

Selena moved closer to the figures, trying to see who they were, but they were faceless shadows going about their duties. One stood off to the side, looking on as the other wrote on the floor. The liquid he used to make the symbols was dark, almost black under the harsh red lighting. It streamed over the floor in rivulets that branched out from a primary source. Selena followed the stream, her stomach twisting as though subconsciously she already knew what that dark liquid would be, yet she gasped when she saw the naked body lying on its side, blood flowing from under it. She didn't want to look, to see who was dead on the floor, but an unknown force drove her forward to take a closer look at the familiar dark curls, the ebony skin she'd known for years. The face frozen, brown eyes opened wide, stared unseeing into the room. Selena's heart stopped, shattering into pieces. Her feet gave out beneath her, and she fell to her knees next to the body of her friend. As though she could feel Selena, Mini took her last breath and whispered, "Love you both."

Selena gasped awake, her face wet with the tears from her nightmare. She sat up on the sofa, pushing back the blanket Shalik had probably covered her with. Reaching for her phone, she checked the time—nine-thirty pm. Mini should have been here by now. Hands shaking, she pulled up her friend's number.

Then she felt it, just like the night of her celebration party. A wave of magic hit her, stealing her breath for a moment.

The door to Shalik's room burst open. He stumbled out dressed in sweats, his blue hair tousled from sleep. "Mini," he whispered.

Selena struggled out from under the blankets, then followed him out the door.

By unspoken agreement, they didn't hurry to where the magic came from. They took the elevator down to the upper floor of the club, then eased their way down to the darkness of the lowest level. Heads tilted, they listened for anything—footsteps on the hard tile, the shifting of fabric—anything that would tell them someone was there. Nothing came out of the dark. Rather than searching for the light, Selena used her magic and sent it out to the mirrors in the room. Each reflective surface lit up with her power, shining over the dead body in the center of the dance floor.

She lay just like she had in Selena's dream. Naked and on her side, facing away from them. The symbols that the being had written surrounded her where she laid lifeless in the middle. Selena didn't need to get closer to know who it was. In fact, she didn't take another step forward. She just sat at the bottom of the stairs as she felt a piece of her heart break off and die. Her eyes stayed fixed on the body even as Shalik moved forward, his steps slow as though in a trance. He fell to his knees beside her, gathered Miniver in his arms, and let out a keening wail as his heart shattered.

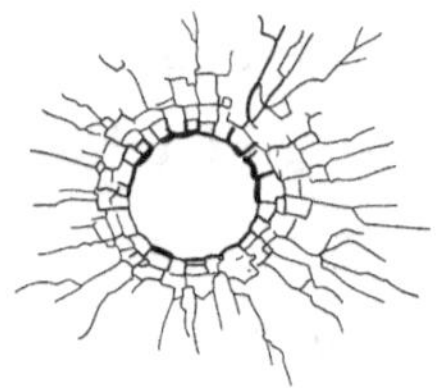

Chapter 20

Mini was dead, and Shalik was heartbroken and sedated in his room. Someone was going to pay. Selena's power surrounded her, crackling like lightning, her eyes a pair of Mercury pools. Everyone cleared a path as she stomped down the street from the club to toward Ofilia's house. Car horns blared, bulbs from streetlights shattering in her wake. Her emotions were a storm manifested into magic. Magic she was going to use to get the truth from Ofilia one way or another.

She didn't bother announcing herself to the doorman of Ofilia's building. Instead, she just blew past him and headed up to Ofilia's level where the elevator opened to the only apartment on the floor. Selena didn't hesitate as she threw her magic. The mirrored doors spelled for protection shattered along with the glass. Selena was stepping over the shards, her boots crunching on them, when Ofilia hurried out of what Selena assumed was her bedroom.

"What is the meaning of this impertinence?" Ofilia demanded. She was dressed in her usual blue robes, hair pulled back, feet bare. The perfect image of innocence. Selena wanted to carve up her lying face. When her power surged, the shards of glass on the floor levitated.

Ofilia released her magic to throw up a white shield. "Selena, I don't know why you're upset, but you're letting your magic rule you."

"Upset? I not upset, Ofilia. I'm fucking furious." Selena whipped her hand forward, and a shard of glass flew toward the shield, dissolving into dust. Selena smirked. "I thought your power was scrying, Ofilia? Where did you learn to shield? Or were you just lying? Like you've been lying about everything else?" Selena threw two more shards, watching them dissolve in the light.

"I've never lied about my power. Scrying is my strongest level. The others are latent, but they've gotten stronger over the years."

"Bullshit. It doesn't matter anyway because once you've confessed about what you did to Mini, I'm going to carve out your lying tongue and then slice the rest of you into very thin pieces."

"What are you talking about?"

"Why d'you have to kill her?" Selena screamed

The shield wavered as Ofilia went two shades paler. She reached out a hand, searching for purchase. There was none, so she simply slid to her knees on the floor. "Minerver's dead?"

"Don't act like you don't know. You did this. She told me she was coming here. She told me she found something at the Salva building, and now she's dead. You killed her because she found something on *you*."

Ofilia looked up from where she landed on the floor. "You think... I killed her?" Tears filled her eyes. "I would never hurt Mini. She was like a daughter to me. She had so much potential, and I thought she might even replace me one day."

"Lies," Selena screamed.

"Selena?" The familiar voice had her shifting her gaze past Ofilia into Alden's citrine eyes.

"What are you doing here?" she demanded.

"I came to collect some papers for Raesean. We've been waiting hours for Mini, but she never showed."

"What?" Doubt and confusion bled through Selena's magical haze.

"Listen to me, Selena," Alden said, moving closer to Ofilia. "We've been here for hours waiting on Mini, trying to call her, but she never showed."

"She never showed," Selena repeated, her voice soft with confusion. "She said she was coming here."

"Yes, she was told to come here to drop of some documents," he said as though talking to a child. "But she never made it. I'm so sorry."

Everything that had been bubbling in Selena came to a head, and she let out a wordless scream. The lights in the room brightened, sparked out, then broke as her power surged outward.

Mirrors throughout the apartment shattered in various rooms. Selena clenched her hands into fists, and every piece of glass her power touched came through walls and doors, heading straight for Ofilia.

"Lena," Alden shouted. The shards came to a sudden halt inches away from Ofilia.

"Selena, I know we've had our differences, but I would never hurt Mini. I only wanted what's best for her, and I only wanted what's best for you. Either of you could have taken my place on the Council. You could have ruled and made things better for everyone. That's all I've ever wanted."

Selena's hand shook as she readied to make the final blow. Tears blinded her eyes, her face contorted in rage. "Ofilia, the only reason I haven't cut you to ribbons is because Alden said Mini wasn't here. But if I find out you had anything to do with her death, I will flay you and make sure you're tortured in the worse part of the Abyss." When she unclenched her hands, the glass rained down, shattering even more on the floor. Selena turned for the door.

"Wait," Ofilia called. "Let me help you find out who did this."

"Forget it," Selena said, kicking a pair of Ofilia's butter-yellow shoes out of her way and heading out the door.

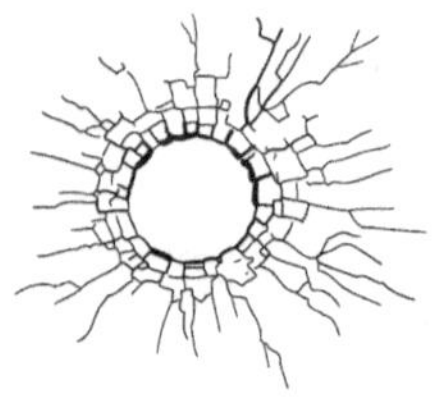

Chapter 21

Selena stumbled out of Ofilia's apartment building. Now that the magic had receded, exhaustion washed over her. Her feet cover the distance over the sidewalk, but they weren't guided in any direction. Even though she'd tucked her magic away, people gave her a wide birth. Her clothes were stained with Mini's blood from when Shalik had gripped it after being forced to relinquish Mini's body. He'd hunched over her, almost feral, when they'd tried to take her away. The enforces had to bring in a mystic to sedate him. Selena had held him as he went under and he'd gripped her sweater like a lifeline to a drowning man.

Anger stirred in her once gain. She was no closer to finding the person who did this, and now one of her friends was dead and she still didn't know what this person wanted. Thunder rumbled, and the skies opened. Fat water droplets rained down on her, but she continued to wonder aimless through the streets of Fusion City.

She didn't hear him at first, over the thunder and the pounding rain. A warm hand rested on her shoulder, halting her forward movement and she turned baring her teeth.

"Easy, Lena, easy." He slipped off his jacket and wrapped it around her.

"Raesean?" She said his name like a question as though what she was seeing wasn't real.

"Yes, Lena, let me take you home," he whispered. Bundling her closer, he hurried her down the street to where his town car waited.

"She's dead, Rae," Selena whispered, a numbness settling over her.

"I know, baby. We'll figure it out." He helped her into the backseat of the car, then got in on the other side.

"Take us to her place, Henry," he told the driver, who'd been waiting with the engine running. The car glided away from the curb, headed to her building. Raesean pulled her into his lap, then placed a gentle kiss on her forehead. She burrowed into his arms, stealing his warmth. She inhaled his usual scent and something more—the undertone of sulfur and burnt red brick.

"You've been to the Abyss," she whispered.

He stiffened, but he didn't move away. "Yes. How did you know?"

"I can smell it. The sulfur," she mumbled, her face still in his neck.

"I'd just came back when I heard the news. I dropped by your apartment. Shalik was there, covered in blood. He said he didn't know where you were."

"I went to kill Ofilia."

"Ah."

"I couldn't do it." The words came out flat.

"I know." He ran a hand over her sopping curls. "It's not in your nature to kill. To torture, maybe, but not kill. Trust me, I'm a demon. I know these things."

Selena scoffed. "Trusting a demon. Isn't that against the rules?"

He remind silent, his hands continued to soothe.

It wasn't long before the driver had pulled over in front of her building. Raesean helped her out of the car. The rain had turned into a light drizzle, and he walked her to the private entrance of her building and pressed the intercom.

Shalik's face showed up and the tiny monitor before the door buzzed open. He was waiting by the open apartment door, Cerberus whining at his feet when they stepped off the elevator.

He pulled her away from Raesean, wrapping his arms around her. "*Don't ever* do that again." His voice was fierce as he spoke to the top of her head. "Never again, Lena. I lost... I lost... I can't lose you, too."

"I'm sorry. I wasn't thinking. I was just so angry. I'm still angry," she said.

Shalik sighed. He looked over at Raesean and mouthed, "Thank you."

Raesean nodded. "Well, I'll be on my way."

Selena pulled away from Shalik.

"Shalik, can you give us a minute?"

Without a word, he trooped back inside, Cerberus following on his heels.

"Thank you."

"Don't thank me. I'm just protecting my interest."

"Huh. I suppose if that's your story." She shrugged.

"It is," he said, face blank.

She nodded, knowing he couldn't allow anyone to find out he'd done something without benefit to him. "Okay, I'll call you tomorrow," she said before turning and walking into the apartment, closing the door behind her.

* * *

She didn't call him the next day. Nor the one after that. Instead, she puttered around the apartment with Shalik. Two broken and wounded animals. One trying to swim above his grief, the other fighting not to unleash her anger and let the world burn. Everything they did was automatic. They performed normal everyday activities without thought, just necessity. Selena didn't know how many days they did this, but as they sat, both pushing their breakfast around their plates, she decided.

"We need to see her."

"What?" Shalik looked up from his plate, his face was drawn from sleepless nights. He'd lost a few pounds from not eating the food he'd prepared. Even his hair had turned a duller shade of blue.

"We need to see her," Selena said again, laying down her fork and leaning back in her chair.

Shalik bowed his head. "I want to. I really want to, but if you go back to the Abyss, there's a chance you may not come back." He looked up, eyes boring into hers. "I can't lose you, too, and Mini wouldn't want you trapped down there."

Selena let out a snort. "She'd be spitting mad."

Shalik smiled, his first real one in days. "Remember the time we broke into that jewelry store to get Mini those earrings she wanted for her birthday?"

She grinned. "Yes, I also remember how she chewed us out for taking such a risk."

"She still wore them, though, every day for weeks."

"Then hocked them so we could have that new couch in our first apartment."

Shalik sighed. "I'm going to miss her. I'm never going to be able to tell her how I feel. She was it for me, and she will never know. Worse, I don't even know where she is in the next world. If I will see her there."

"That's why we need to see her."

"Lena..."

"I'm not going to the Abyss," she said, cutting him off. "I'm going to bring the Abyss to me."

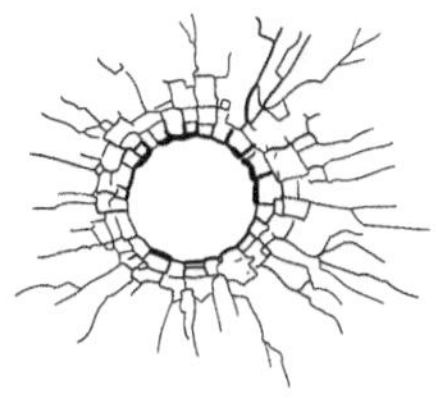

Chapter 22

The plan was simple. Abaddon's home was at the center of the Abyss. In it were several mirrors she could use like a GPS to find him. Once she knew where he was, Selena's plan was to have a chat with the ruler of the Abyss and politely ask him to tell her where Mini was. It remained to be seen—despite their turbulent history—if he would cooperate.

"Are you sure about this?" Shalik asked, his voice laced with worry. Selena had successfully avoided Abaddon for years. Now she was about to reveal herself to him.

"Yes," she confirmed. "We can't move forward unless we know she's at peace. That she's in the Fields of Asphodel."

He nodded. "But I'm staying by your side the entire time."

"Okay, just don't say anything."

"Okay."

They'd moved the center table out of the way and now sat on the rug into front of the wall-to-wall windows. Cerberus snored softly in his cage. With a quick glance, she doubled checked that it was out of the sight from the windows she was about to use. When she was sure, she leaned forward and laid her index finger on the glass, sending a thread of magic through. The windows clouded much like her eyes when she used her powers, mercury spilling over its surface, the glass turning from windows to mirrors.

"I never get over how you can do that," Shalik murmured, his voice almost reverent.

She let out a breath. "That's the simple part." She picked up the knife she'd sat down with and pricked her finger. Blood welled at the tip. She used it to draw the symbols for the spell to call Abaddon.

The mirrors shimmered, showing various reflections. Some of hallways while others were of demons performing their torturous duties. Selena quickly blanked those until finally she found him.

He was at his desk in his office, looking over a pile of documents. He looked up when he sensed her magic, his eyes locked with hers in the mirror he had on the far wall opposite his desk. He leaned back in his chair, angling himself toward her.

"Well, this is an unexpected surprise." He laced his fingers together over his stomach.

"Abaddon, it's been a while." Selena's face was the picture of calm even though her insides churned.

"Yes…" He paused, head tilting as though thinking. "I haven't seen you since I sent you to collect a much-needed soul and you never returned. Next thing I knew, I was short one Charon, one terrible soul, and the Guardian to the gates of the Underworld."

"Cerberus was my dog, and he wanted to come with me."

Abaddon sat up in his chair, slamming his palm on the top of his desk. "He is not a pet."

"Oh really?" Selena arched a brow. "Is that why you had a bowl of treats for him in your bottom desk drawer?"

"I don't know what you're talking about." He sniffed. "Anyway, to what do I owe this call? Have you finally come to you senses and are ready to come home?"

Selena felt Shalik stiffen beside her.

"No. I need a favor," she mumbled.

"Say that again. I didn't quite catch that," he said with a grin.

She rolled her eyes. "I need to see someone."

"What do I get in return for granting you this favor?"

"What do you want?"

"You know what I want," he said, his face serious.

"I can't give you that. Anything else?" She folded her arms over her chest.

"A visit home for one week. With..." he said, stopping her before she could say anything, "any stipulations or qualifiers you want."

"A day,"

"Five days."

"Three."

"Deal. I'd shake on it, but mirror and all." He shrugged. "Now, what do you want?"

"I want to see a soul."

"Oh, did you send me someone to punish?" His voice was that of a person opening a present they'd been wanting for years.

"No! I want to see if a soul made it to the Fields of Asphodel."

"Absolutely not! Souls there are not to be disturbed."

"We don't want to talk to her. We just want to see if she's there and if she's happy."

"Selena..."

"Father, please."

Maybe it was the tears in her voice or the fact she called him 'Father,' something she rarely did, but he sighed.

"Open a portal," he said. He stood, moving closer to the mirror.

"No." Shalik wrapped his fingers around her wrist to stop her from moving.

"Well, how else is she going to get the blood?" Abaddon hissed.

"Blood?" Shalik whispered.

"If you don't know what she's got to do, then bloody well shut up," Abaddon snapped.

Selena laid her free hand on Shalik's thigh to quiet him. When she looked at him, he released her hand. Turning back to the mirror, she drew a circle wide enough for Abaddon to slip his hand through. Selena picked up the knife she'd used previously, then pricked her father's finger. Blood welled. He turned his wrist over, then pinched three drops into her palm.

"That's all you need," he said gruffly, pulling his hand back over to his side.

"Thank you." She cradled her bloody hand to her chest.

Dipping her finger in it, Selena drew the symbol she needed to channel Abaddon's power to view into the mystic realm. The mirror split so that one half was of Abaddon, and the other looked like a pool of mercury. Adding one more symbol, she clasped Shalik's hand and said, "Think of Mini. Think of what you desire."

The mirror shimmered, then an image formed like a movie. In the mirror, sunlight streamed down over blue irises and there Mini stood. Her magic floated water up from a nearby source, then released it to shower lightly over the flowers. She smiled, looking down at the droplets on the petals.

"There," she said. "Now you have tiny mirrors to reflect all that blue."

Selena's hand tightened in Shalik's, her eyes filling with tears.

"She always loved tending flowers," Shalik whispered. "But she never could in the city, never had the time."

"Now," Mini said to the flowers. "I'll be back to chat with you after I've tended the others. Then I can tell you all about my two best friends."

With a last soft touch to a petal, she moved on to the other flowers.

"Sir, you..."

The voice that came through the mirror from Abaddon's office had Selena shifting her gaze. Raesean stood there, eyes wide, darting between the split mirror and Abaddon.

"Sir, if you're busy, I can come back."

"No, unless Selena would like to take up her duties."

"No." Her tone was unmoving.

"Fine." Abaddon shrugged.

She reached over to clear the mirror.

"Ah," he said before she could blank the mirror. "I expect to see you soon."

"Not too soon." She sent a pulse of magic to dismantle the spell, then cleared all the mirrors until they returned to the regular bank of windows.

Selena turned Shalik, throwing her arms around him. "She's okay."

Shalik squeezed her tight. His body gave one hard shudder before relaxing as he rocked her from side to side. "She okay," he whispered over and over. "She's okay, and she's happy."

"Yes," Selena agreed, filled with mixed emotions.

Selena now had another problem to deal with, though. She knew without question Raesean would soon be on her doorstep, demanding answers. The question was if he had figured out Abaddon was her father, and, if he had, what would he want to keep that information to himself?

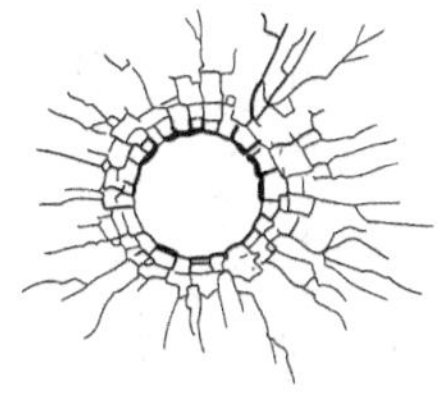

Chapter 23

Selena sighed at the loud banging on the door. Sometimes, she hated being right. In this case, though, it helped her prepare for the angry demon outside her door. The banging increased, but she continued to ignore it, a part of her hoping he would give up.

Shalik stepped out his room in a dark green hoodie, sweats, and sneakers. His wet hair hung wet over his shoulder. He'd done something to make the blue brighter, and he stood pulling it back in to a ponytail.

"Are you going to deal with that?" He leaned a shoulder against the doorjamb.

"I'm thinking about it," she said from her sprawled position on the sofa, her eyes on the ceiling.

"Well, I'm heading out for a run and taking Cerberus with me. I need to clear my head."

Translation: he wanted to think about seeing Mini and not deal with all the drama that came with the demon outside. He scooped Cerberus's leash off the top of his cage, then opened the door for him to scamper out. The bundle of fur launched out, barking and jumping up on his hind legs. Shalik scooped him up as he headed for the front door. Selena climbed off the sofa to follow him with a huff. He threw open the door to find Raesean's hands raised to bang on it again. His arm froze mid-knock, and he glared first at Shalik and then at Selena, who stood a few paces behind.

"How did you even get through the private entrance?" Selena demanded.

"I picked the lock."

"And the spell?"

"I told you I'm not here to harm you, although I might definitely throttle you if you don't answer my questions."

Shalik shook his head and walked out the door, a barking Cerberus in hand.

"Be careful," Selena shouted at his back as he headed for the elevator.

She turned her focus to the demon, then waved him in.

He stepped over the threshold, deliberately closing the door behind him. The soft click as it snapped in place might as well been a loud slam as the demon stared. His body was tense, his fingers clenching and unclenching.

"What game are you playing at, Selena?" He took a slow step forward.

"Look, not that it's any of your business, but I needed something from Abaddon, okay?"

"You... you made a deal with *him*?" he whispered

"Of a sort. A favor for a favor. Does it matter?" she challenged.

"Did you have qualifiers?" He took another step closer to her.

"Of course I did. I'm not stupid."

Raesean let out a relieved breath, then his brow furrowed. "How do you even know Abaddon? Are you lovers?"

She gagged, fighting back the onslaught of bile that rose in her throat at the thought. "Definitely not."

"Then..."

"I work for him." She cut him off before he could start speculating more. The last thing she needed was for him to find out Abaddon was her father.

"You work for him?"

"Yes. Well, at least I did. I'm a Charon."

"You're a boatman?"

"We prefer our correct title of Charon,"

Raesean's confusion was written all over his face. Selena sighed. "Look, I *was* a Charon. Aba sent me up here to pick up a soul. I bailed, and I haven't been back since. He's still pissed about it, and he's trying to get me back to work."

"What do you mean by you bailed?"

"As in quit the job." She looked at him as though he were stupid.

"You can't just quit a job the leader of the Underworld has given you." His voice was laced with exasperation.

"Yeah, well…" Selena turned away from him, then made her way over to the sofa. She knew she had to be careful with what she said next. Otherwise, the story she'd just been building would fall apart. "When I took the job, I requested free will." She shrugged. "He granted it, but it backfired when I left the job. Now he can't force me back to work."

Raesean joined her on the sofa. "So… you're not dead, and you're not going back to the Abyss?"

Selena giggled. "You thought I was dead?"

He nodded, his face serious. "For a split second, when I walked in and saw you in the mirror, I thought you were dead and trapped there."

"What—were you worried about me?" she scoffed.

Something shifted in his eyes. She couldn't tell what it was, but before she could figure it out, he'd closed the distance between them, slipped his hand into her hair, and pressed his lips to hers.

Selena jerked, but he'd obviously expected it, firmly holding her head while he rubbed his lips against hers. His lips were soft but firm, and he ran his tongue over her lips, asking permission, wanting her to open for him. Slowly, she did, and he slipped his tongue inside. The kiss deepened, heated, and Selena let go—of her worry over keeping her secret, her anger at her friend's murder, and her fear the killer would kill someone else she cared about. Instead, she placed her focus on the demon she'd been attracted to for years.

Selena slipped her hands under his suit jacket, then ran them over his shirt-clad abs. His muscles jumped under her fingers, but he made no move to stop her. She took that as an invitation, pulling his shirt out of his pants so she could touch skin. He groaned, reciprocating by running his free hand up her sides and cupping her breast. When she gasped, Raesean tilted his head to take more of her mouth. Her control slipped. She gripped the two sides of his shit and pulled. Buttons popped, plopping to the carpeted floor. Her hands connected with bare skin, and she pushed at his muscular chest. He gave way, pulling away from her as he laid back, eyes riveted as she climbed on top of him. She moaned when she felt the hard length of him between them. She wanted to divest him of every stitch of clothing he wore. To feel his skin against hers. To have him run his hands and lips over her body, but first she wanted to slide her tongue over every ridge and bump of his abs and chest.

She shifted her body until she was kneeling between his thighs, then leaned over and planted a soft kiss above his belly button. His muscles flexed in response, and she smiled. Ever so slowly, she made her way up his chest, licking and biting along the way. He groaned, wrapping his hands around her waist and repositioning her on top of him. He skimmed his hand upward, bunching the fabric of her t-shirt until she removed it.

Raesean took in the glory of her body. The copper skin, the pert breasts that were a handful and the tiny waist that he could wrap both hands around. He once again took her mouth, then glided his hands lower to the top of her leggings.

A small bundle of fur jumped on them. Selena slid sideways, falling to the floor with a thump.

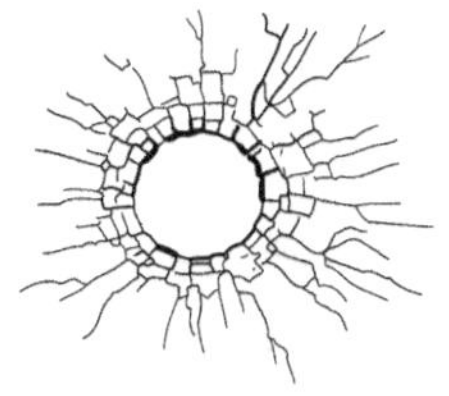

Chapter 24

Cerberus' tongue worked double time to lick everywhere he could reach. His body vibrated in joy as he climbed all over her. "Cerberus..." She giggled, trying to push the dog off her. "Stop, Cerberus."

"Don't blame the dog for wanting to lick you," Raesean murmured, discreetly adjusting himself. He looked down at his ruined shirt and buttoned his suit jacket over it as Shalik approached the sofa, eyes darting between them.

"Looks like I got here just in time," he said with a pointed look at Selena.

"I don't know what you're talking about. We were just discussing some things." Selena buried her face in Cerberus's fur as she stood, dog in her arms.

"Sure..." Shalik picked up a stray button from the back of the couch. "Yours, I believe," he said, handing the button to Raesean, who, for the first time in all the years she'd known him, flushed.

Shalik smirked, turning his attention back to Selena as she placed Cerberus back in his cage. "In your discussion, did you ask him if he knew anything about the pit?"

Now it was Selena's turn to fight back embarrassment while she locked the cage door. "I was just getting around to it."

"The pit?" Raesean said. "What about the pit?"

Selena and Shalik turned to him. "You know what the pit is?" Shalik demanded.

"Yes, it's where the demons used to do sacrifices before Abaddon put a stop to it over a century ago. What does the pit have to do with anything?"

"It was the last thing Mini told us about," Shalik said. "She said she found something out, then asked us to talk to you about it."

"Where did she find this information?" His brow furrowed, eyes curious.

"In the Salva building. She called from there the day she..." Selena swallowed. "The day she died."

He glanced at his watch. "Well, I can go to the Salva building to see what I can find out. Or we can head over to the pit to see if we can find anything there. Your call."

"Let's go to the pit," Selena blurted. Something in her gut told her that this was where Mini had died. Maybe they could find something there on the person who was committing all these murders.

Raesean stood, pulling his cell phone out of his inner jacket pocket. "Let me make a call, then we can head over there to see if we find anything."

"Where is there?" Shalik questioned.

"Westside. A few blocks from my club, actually."

"Of course." Shalik's voice dripped sarcasm.

"Problem?" Raesean arched a brow, his smile taunting.

"Okay, that's enough, boys." Stepping between them, she held a hand up. "Rae, make the call and I'll come with you."

He looked down at her, his eyes softening. With a nod, he walked out of the apartment to make his call in the hallway.

"I don't like this, Selena." Shalik folded his fingers together over his chest.

She waved her hand. "It's nothing. I'll just take a quick trip there to see what's what. If we find anything, I'll call Enforcer Draykon."

"That's not the only thing I don't like," he said, nodding his head in the direction Raesean had gone.

She opened her mouth to protest, but he cut her off. "You can't stand there topless, your headlights on high beam, and tell me there's nothing going on between you two."

She glanced down. To her embarrassment, she realized she'd been walking around with no shirt.

She scrambled over the back of the sofa to grab the t-shirt she'd removed earlier. "Look..."

"No, you look." He laid a hand on her shoulder. "I don't care that you have the hots for the one demon you should stay away from. And it's clear he has feelings for you."

"He doesn't."

He tightened the grip on her shoulder. "It doesn't matter. What's important is that we focus on finding a killer who is leaving dead bodies for you as threats. Dead bodies with old demon symbols. Now, the representative of the demons is saying they have an old sacrificial pit. A pit Mini warned us about before she was murdered." He gave her a shoulder a little shake. "We can't trust any demon until we sort this out, Selena."

She nodded. "Okay, but I still want take look at it."

"Then let's go."

"No, Shalik. You can't go with me."

"Yes, I can." He shook his head.

"I need you here in case something happens, and you have to send in the enforcers."

"Why not take them in the first place?"

"For one thing, Raesean would laugh in my face if I suggested it. Also, we have no evidence that it's connected in any way. How will I explain how I know about it and what the demons used to use it for?"

He closed his eyes.

"It's fine. I'll take my phone with me. You can track me though my GPS. If I don't call you in two hours, you can contact Draykon." Selena raised a hand to his face, and he leaned into it. "It's gonna be okay, Li. One way or another, we're going to get to the bottom of this."

He let out a breath slowly. "Promise me that if anything happens, you'll use your magic."

"I don't..."

He squeezed her shoulder tighter. "Promise me. Do whatever it takes to survive, even if you have to burn everything to the ground and send everyone to the Abyss. I don't care what you have to do. Survive, Selena."

There was a knock at the front door, and Raesean poked his head back in.

"Ready?"

"Let me get my phone and some shoes."

"And your necklace," Shalik reminded her.

Their eyes met, and she gave him a small nod before hurrying to her room. Once she was back, her gaze darted between Raesean and Shalik. The tension between them was think enough for her to walk on.

"Everything okay?" Selena questioned.

Raesean didn't bother to answer. He just said, "Alden will meet us there with the keys. Let's go."

"All right," she drawled.

With a last look at Shalik, she turned and walked out the door.

* * *

They sat silently in the back of his black town car, each staring out their respective windows.

"We have to talk about it eventually," he said, his gaze locked on the scenery passing outside.

"I know," she agreed

"But not now?" The words came out as a question.

"No, after we find out who's been killing the people I care about."

"Fair enough. But I must warn you, this thing between us isn't over, Selena."

She turned to find him watching her intensely. "We'll talk after this mess is over."

He shifted his gaze out the window once again.

The car pulled up to a decrepit building. The windows were boarded up, and most of the paint had abandoned the building like everything else.

Not everything, Selena thought as Raesean helped her out of the car. The scent of mold and piss wafted up her nose. When she wrinkled her face in displeasure, he chuckled.

"I told you we haven't used this place in years."

"Actually, you said a century ago," she muttered, tugging on the ends of her t-shirt.

"The pit hasn't been used, but the building had been for various things. I had to abandon it when naughty demons continued to disobey our master's request." His eyes flashed with a dangerous glint.

"I see you have your master's love of punishment."

He grinned. "I like all forms of punishment, especially in the bedroom."

Selena looked away from the heat in his eyes, and he leaned down to whisper in her ear. "You can't avoid what's between us."

She didn't respond, but she let him take her hand to lead her closer to the building. Alden stood by the door, keys in his fist. His face was a blank mask, but his fingers tightened around the keychain.

"Alden," she said, "we must stop meeting in these question-able places."

He shook himself as though coming out of a trance, then smiled. "It's not my fault you like to frequent the questionable and the dangerous." His gaze shifted quickly to Raesean before returning. "So, what brings you to this particular chateau? Have you given up the high life to return to your dark ways?"

"Not exactly," she murmured.

"Pity." He turned, shoved the key in the lock, and twist-ed. The tumbles landed with a thump and an echo. The door swung open on well-oiled hinges.

"That's strange," Raesean commented.

"What is?" she asked.

"Nothing," he murmured, shaking his head.

Alden handed Raesean a flashlight, and the trio trooped in with Raesean in the lead and Alden bringing up the rear. It was dark, and Selena could only see by the dim lights of the flashlights. Cobwebs hung everywhere, and the rats had made themselves at home. Their squeaks echoed off the walls as they moved about the building. White sheets covered unused furniture, and dust motes danced in the flashlight's beam.

Raesean wasted no time in making a beeline for the rear of the room where double doors hung open and askew on their joints. He shined his light past the doors into the other room, then stepped in. It was empty. Not abandoned like the previous ones they'd just walked through, but empty and cleaned. No cobwebs, no dust, nothing. Just an empty space with a huge circular hole in the ground. Selena walked closer to the pit to stare down into the darkness.

"Raesean, for an abandoned building, this room sure is clean."

"I noticed," he said. He walked around the pit, still guiding the light around the room.

"Any idea who has been doing spring cleaning?"

"No, but I'm going to find... *Humph*."

Selena looked up in time to see Raesean's flashlight bob as he fell backward into the pit, the light illuminating the tunnel walls before blinking out. Before she could even react, Selena felt herself go airborne, her arms searching for purchase as she free-fell into the darkness.

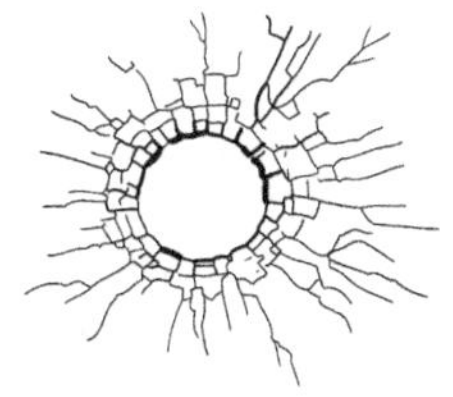

Chapter 25

Selena laid on the cold concrete floor as pain radiated all over her body. She couldn't tell where one injury began and the other ended. When she shifted, her vision went white as pain traveled up her leg. She gritted her teeth as she swallowed back a scream. She wasn't sure how long she laid there, but when she'd finally caught her breath, she glanced down only to see her ankle twisted at an odd angle. After a deep slow breath, she released it. If she didn't get up, she was going to die there.

With some effort, she ground her hands into the uneven floor and pushed up, each movement an effort as she tried and failed not to jar the broken ankle. Sweat gathered on her brow, and she clenched her teeth so hard she thought they would crack. Once upright, she breathed through the pain until it was calmed to a dull roar.

Selena looked around. She was in a pit—not just any pit but the one supposedly out of commission for sacrifices. It was twenty feet wide and circular, the walls so smooth no one could climb out once thrown in. The smell of old blood and other unpleasant stuff filled her nose, making her gag.

Out of commission, my ass

She covered her nose with the back of her hand, breathing through her mouth as she continued her scan of the dimly lit room. Worthless red lighting did nothing to eliminate the deep shadows, so she cocked her head sideways, listening. Electricity buzzed in the ten-watt bulbs. Under the noise, she could hear someone's ragged breathing.

The breathing turned into a cough, and she peered in the noise's direction. Chains rattled, fabric rubbing against the floor as the unknown person sat up. The cough subsided to a dull wheezing. Selena waited, not wanting to let the person know she was there until she could determine if they were friend or foe. She needn't have worried, though, as the voice that called out told her exactly who she was with.

"The last thing I expected was to wake up in the pit with you today, Selena." Raesean shifted, chains clanging at his movement.

"Trust me," she gritted out, her ankle still shouting its displeasure. "It wasn't on my list of thing to do either."

He chuckled, the deep tone merging with the echo in the empty space. "I'm glad to see you've kept that witty disposition of yours, although I don't think it'll help much where we're going."

Selena froze. "What do you mean by where we're going?"

"He means you're going to The Abyss."

The voice seemed to come from nowhere, bouncing around the room. A few feet from where she sat, the shadows gathered upon themselves until a complete black circle formed.

Selena felt icy fingers of fear crawl up her spine as Alden stepped out of the shadows, but her stomach turned to lead when she saw Ofilia with him, one armed linked with his, the other clutching a small bag. The shadows dissipated after they stepped through. The remnants of the symbols he'd written remained on the wall. The pair stared back.

"Ofilia?" Selena whispered.

The smile Ofilia gave Selena was anything but friendly. "Surprised to see me?" Her tone turned mocking while she repeated the words she'd said the night Selena came to kill her. "I would never hurt Mini. I only wanted what's best for her, and I only wanted what's best for you, too."

"You lying bitch," Selena screamed, lunging for the woman. She collapsed back as her ankle delivered another bout of pain.

Ofilia laughed, all traces of innocence and propriety gone. Only the leech that she was remained. She'd donned a crotch-length electric blue dress that look painted on. Her hair was no longer pulled back in a tamed roll. Instead, it fell free in loose waves around her shoulder. She'd done her makeup in drastic contrast, shadowing her eyes in black and dark blues while her lips were a screaming red. The matching blue heels she wore clicked against the icy floor as she stepped closer to Selena.

Selena stared at the shoes, remembering the butter-yellow ones she'd kicked on the way out of Ofilia's apartment that night. The shoes that perfectly matched Mini's purse.

A myriad of thoughts flew through Selena's mind. "Mini came to you that night. She found out you were the killer, and she confronted you."

"Actually, she hadn't quite made that leap yet. She thought it was a rogue demon, and that I could help her stop them. Pity, she was such a brilliant assistant."

"I should have sliced you to ribbons," Selena gritted out.

Ofilia tsked "Oh, dear child, you're not looking your usual perky self."

"Why are you doing this?"

"Because you, my lovely mirror witch," she said as she squatted to Selena's eye level, "are my payment to the Dark One so I can rule all of Fusion City."

Ofilia must have seen Selena's confusion because she continued. "Oh, come now, boatman. I know Abaddon has been looking for you since you abandoned your job of carrying souls. I plan to make a deal with him. I'll give you to him in exchange for him forcing you to transfer your power to me."

"I can't give you my power, Ofilia." Selena shifted again, hoping to get closer to Ofilia to wrap her hands around the bitch's slender throat. "But even if I could, I wouldn't."

"Of course you will," Ofilia said with a dismissive wave. "Abaddon will make you."

Raesean laughed, and Ofilia's face contorted in disgust as she stood to face him. "What's so funny, demon?"

Raesean's chains rattled as he struggled to control his laughter. "That you went through all this trouble to rule and you'll never get to."

"Oh, please... who's going to stop me?" Ofilia smirked, stalking even closer to him, but stopping in the center of the pit. "You?"

"If you're too stupid to know, then I'm not gonna tell you."

Ofilia opened her mouth to respond. Before she could say anything else, Alden was in front of her, raking his claws across her throat. Her eyes widened in surprise, her hand lifting to cover the blood that spurted from her throat.

"Never trust a demon, especially one who has gone rogue," Raesean whispered as Ofilia's body slid to the floor with a thump.

Selena trembled as she watched the blood spreading all over the floor. Alden didn't bat an eye as he trudged through the blood toward her.

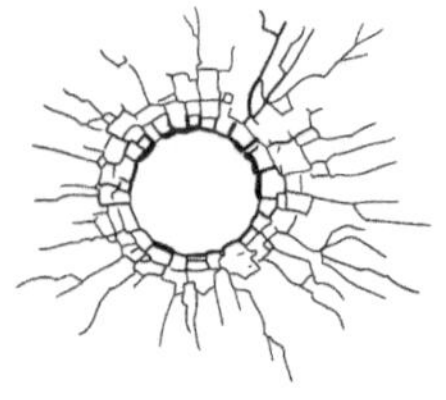

Chapter 26

"That's better." Alden wiped the blood splatter from his face. "I swear her constant prattling would make me slit her throat." He chuckled. "Oh wait, too late."

Selena's eyes darted between the body on the ground and Alden.

"Don't look so upset. I did you a favor by getting rid of her. Besides, would you have preferred she stole your powers and left you in the Abyss?"

Selena peered into his face, seeing nothing but a demon who had lost a few marbles. "What do you want from me?"

His smile was cold and wicked. "I'm so glad you ask. Let's make a deal."

He turned, walking back to Ofilia's body. Kneeling, he dipped a finger in her blood, then began drawing symbols on the ground. "I'll help you with your little Abyss problem," he said absently, "and you can have me as your righthand man."

He glanced up when she remained silent. "Maybe we can eventually be more than that, when you're ready."

Bile rose to her throat as she realized what Alden wanted.

"Oh, don't look that way. I know you have a penchant for demon. What's one over the other?"

Raesean chuckled again. "That you can say that straight-faced tells me that your ego's tiny."

Alden hissed, but he continued to draw the symbols on the ground. "Talk all you want, Raes, but after I'm done here, your ego won't be an option anymore."

Selena ignored them, allowing their snapping to give her more time to figure a way out. There had to be a way to escape without making a deal with a demon. But Alden was steadily drawing those symbols. Her skin broke out in a cold sweat when she realized what they were for. He was going to teleport them to Abaddon.

"Why would I need your help with the Abyss?" she asked, hoping to distract him.

He didn't even pause before he responded. "Don't play coy. I've been telling you along that I know you secret, who..." He went still, head tilting to the side as he considered Raesean, taking the demon's measure.

"Alden, I think you're mistaken. I'm just a Charon. I didn't want the job. It's why I left."

He turned back to Selena, hands covered in blood. "Quit hiding. We both know who you are." He sighed. "Everyone wants more power. The power to rule, to take control of their life, to change the world. It's all the same. The only difference is that *you* can seize your power, and I'm going to help you do it." He dipped his finger in more of Ofilia's blood, then went back to drawing the symbols.

A shiver of horror ran through her as the pieces of the puzzle fell into place. Alden didn't want to help her rule—he wanted to rule The Abyss through her.

Selena dragged herself farther away from the markings. Her leggings snagged on the rough concrete, ripping a hole, her exposed skin scraping and bleeding on the rough floor. But she didn't stop. She needed to not only put some distance between her and his ravings, but also to lean her back against the wall.

She'd taken longer than she'd thought to move herself because when she turned back, he was halfway finished with the circle of power. He'd paid her no mind, his focus solely on his work.

"What are you going to do with the circle once it's done?" she asked innocently, hoping to stall him a bit.

Alden paused his writing to scoff before continuing. "I think you've already figured it out, and you want to stall me to save Raes. Really, Selena, I thought you would be past such earthly emotions. Then again, you did choose the pixie over me. I suppose I should have known better, but I think I can indulge you. You know I won't complete the circle until you've agreed to place me as your righthand man. Then all you have to do is transfer Raesean's power to me. We head down to the Abyss with Raesean's power and you as a gift, and Abaddon will make me his second. I'll take control of his armies, and then The Abyss will be ripe for the picking."

"What a stupid plan," Raesean commented. "You can't rule The Abyss unless you're blood. They'll never accept you."

Alden's laugh was wild, crazed. "Don't worry, I have a queen in the deck."

"I can't transfer his power to you Alden. I don't have that gift."

"You're lying," he snapped. "Ofilia and I have watched you closely over the years. We know your power level is closer to a level nine, maybe even a ten. If you're that high, higher than Ofilia, you would have the highest-level power. You would have the power of the reincarnated mirror witch."

Selena said no more. She couldn't make him see the truth because, like most desperate people, he would believe what he wanted. So she left him to finish the circle while she slipped her necklace off. Removing the pendant, she crushed it, holding the fragments in her hand.

"There," he said in satisfaction. "It took a while, but luckily I had practice."

"How do I know you won't double cross me?" she asked.

He smiled. "Because, just like you, I want things to change. I want life to be better for beings who weren't born with high-level powers. Together, with an army from the Abyss, we can make it so. Overthrow the humans and the higher powered who seek to cowl us."

"Okay," she agreed.

Alden smiled.

"But I can't transfer the power without a mirror," she pointed out, knowing what he would do next.

"Oh, we came prepared." When he reached down to pick up Ofilia's blood-soaked bag, Selena blew the fragments of her crushed mirror necklace toward him. By the time Alden had pulled the mirror out of Ofilia's bag, Selena had already released her magic, directing the fragments to hover around him. The light from her magic reflected on the tiny particles forming a white shield around Alden.

He looked around, eyes wide, hands holding the mirror like a lifeline. "What are you doing, Selena?"

"People never listen when I tell them that I can't do what they ask." She raised her hand to direct the full force of her magic toward him. Her body glowed as the magic pulsed through her. "It's like whatever they think they know about me is true." The light bulbs in the room popped one after the other as her anger took hold. More magic pumped through her, escaping her body in fractured light, illuminating the entire pit.

"Selena, stop. You can't do this. We had a deal." He banged his fist against the shield.

"No, we didn't. We never shook on it. But you were right about one thing," she replied, ignoring his cries. "I am the mirror witch, but I don't transfer magic into my mirrors."

"Wh-what do you do?" he stammered.

"I trap souls," she whispered.

Alden started to sweat. As though realizing what she was going to do, he threw down the mirror and the hope he'd been clinging to. Selena seized control of the falling glass. She levitated it up so he could look into it. His eyes went wide when he saw his reflection. With that one look, Selena unleashed the full force of her magic, pulling Alden's soul from his body and putting it into the mirror. His body slumped to the floor while his soul screamed from behind the glass.

"Say hello to Abaddon for me," she shouted at him before dismantling her shield, using the bloody fragments to form the symbols and complete the blood circle. The light of her power traveled throughout the remaining symbols, turning the circle into a mirrored pool, and the two bodies sank smoothly into it. Selena released her magical grip on the mirror containing Alden's soul. She watched it follow his body, screaming all the way. When the portal surface was smooth again, she shut down the outpouring of magic until she no longer glowed.

Her breath heaved, exhaustion washing over her as she collapsed on her side, unable to move. In the dark, she heard the soft shifting of chains. Just before she passed out, Raesean's whisper floated to her.

"What the fuck just happened?"

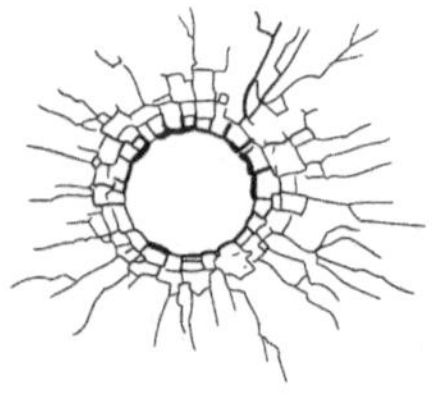

Chapter 27

Selena sat on a bench near the Salva building, waiting for Raesean to show after he'd demanded this meeting. It had been several months since her encounter with the high-level demon. Her leg had healed enough that she could wobble about with a cane without Shalik hovering like a bloody nanny and demanding she drink more of his nasty vegetable mix. She told him she'd already battled a demon, and she didn't need more reminders of things from the Abyss.

Although she groused, she was still grateful to be alive. Truth was that if it weren't for Shalik calling the enforcers when he hadn't heard from her in the allotted time, the rats would probably be gnawing on hers and Raesean's body at this very moment.

She shuddered at the thought, then stretched her injured leg out, relaxing her back into the curve of the bench. The nearby trees rustled as the wind wove through them. Sunshine warmed her copper skin, and she raised her face toward the heat. Her power thrummed, and the sunlight refracted off every exposed inch, warming her even more.

She closed her eyes, letting out a contented sigh.

"You really shouldn't do that in a public setting."

Selena didn't even bother to open her eyes, knowing full well the demon had been following her since she'd hopped into a taxi from her home.

"I only did it because I knew you wouldn't be able to resist showing yourself if I did." With another sigh, she pulled her power in. "What is that you want, Raesean? Are you here to demand that I close my business, test to find out the true level of my power, or..." This time, she opened her eyes and stared directly into his pale blue ones. He stood behind the bench, gazing at her upturned face. "Did your master send you to collect me?"

Raesean walked around the bench, then settled in next to her. "I haven't come to collect you for... my master. I see no reason to. The removal of a rogue demon working with a member of the Council to overthrow the powers-that-be is not something that would upset him. Especially as he was gifted the demon's soul *and* body to punish."

Selena shuddered as the implication of what Alden was going through manifested in her mind. If Abaddon had figured out how to put the soul back in the body, Alden was likely begging for death at this point. She couldn't help but feel pity for the misguided being. "So, what are your plans exactly, Raesean? And you've yet to address the club or the testing."

He sat quietly, gaze focused on the building. They sat in uneasy silence.

"It's not every day I owe someone a life debt." He paused again as though weighing his words. His feet shifted slightly on the grass below. That slight movement might as well have been him clearing his throat with nerves. But he went on. "After your little display that night, I did some research on your power and your... lineage."

Selena stiffened, her hand reaching for her necklace.

He lifted his hands in an easy-does-it gesture. "Let me finish."

"The direction your words are taking isn't doing anything to make me want to let you finish, Raesean." Her body tensed, ready to yank the pendant from around her neck. Power began building in her.

"I plan to leave you be," he said in a rush.

Slowly, Selena relaxed, letting out a slow breath. "Explain."

"I find myself in the oddest predicament of owing you a life debt. Considering your lineage, it may not be a good idea to piss you off so early in the game. You don't consider mercy when crossed." He gave her a mirthless smirk.

She arched a brow. "I don't have the luxury of mercy, as you well know."

"Yes, I do, which is why I've decided to leave you be. If any-one asks, I was unconscious through the events of that night. Therefore, I'm unaware of exactly what happened." He turned his gaze to the building in front of him and kept his focus there, hands interlocked, knuckles white. "Whatever story you tell is what will be on the record. Also, you don't have to take the test again. That was mostly Ofilia's hang-up, anyway. I will sign off on the completion of Shalik's indentureship, too. If you continue to pay your business dues, then your license will automatically renew. As a matter of fact, anything needing to be completed in the Salva building can be done by mail or via proxy."

For a moment, she sat with her mouth agape, not able to believe what she'd heard. Then she remembered who she was talking to. There was always a price when dealing with a demon. She snapped her mouth closed and eyed him, waiting for the other shoe to drop. "That's mighty generous of you, Rae. But what do you want from me in exchange?"

"Nothing."

She frowned at his response. "What?"

"I want absolutely nothing from you. In fact, I would prefer never to see you again, Selena Decland. So, the deal is that I'll leave you be, and you shall never grace the halls of the Salva building or my neck of the woods again."

"Sounds like you want to pretend this never happened."

Now he faced her, shoulders tight with anger. "You think I'm stupid? I know who you are and what you're expected to do. I don't want to get between you and my boss because whether you'd like to admit it or not, things are coming to a head between you two. Should the shit hit the fan, I want plausible deniability if he asks any questions."

"Ha." Her laugh was bitter. "There is no denying anything when it comes to him, Raesean. One way or another, he always gets his way."

He stood, adjusting the jacket of his designer suit. "Then consider this the first gift of your reign, my lady."

Without out another word, he walked away, heading into the Salva building. Selena watched him go. Minutes later, Shalik appeared by her side. He had left home before her to check out the meeting place just in case it was an ambush. In his words, he was taking no chances.

"How'd it go?" he asked

She smiled. "Better than I thought. Apparently, he doesn't want anyone to know he owes me a life debt, so he is content to give me everything I want and leave me be in exchange. I live my life, he lives his, and we all get along."

Shalik laughed. "Well, that's splendid news, isn't it?"

"Yup," she agreed. "Now, lucky penny," she teased, referring to the new nickname she'd given him after all she'd been through. "Help us get a taxi home. You know I'll never get another miracle again today without you present."

Arms linked, the pair walked toward the park exit. Although she laughed and joked with him, the cold hard pit of fear that had lodged in her stomach after Raesean's declaration didn't go away. Life was about to change drastically. Selena's only hope was that she survived the unspoken battle between her and the ruler of the Abyss.

* * *

Continue the Demons and Souls series in book two coming soon.

dhgibbs.com

* * *

Newsletter

Click here to sign up.

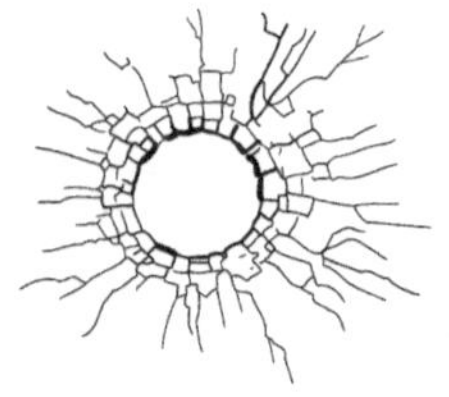

Epilogue

Flames danced over Raesean's fingertips as he walked through the blood and glass on the floor. His shoes sounded like he was walking on sandpaper with each step he took. Whenever he came to a demon that had already returned to the Abyss, he dropped a spark on it to ensure nothing of the body remained.

He chuckled to himself, glancing around at the carnage. Selena might think she's above the demons, but she has a temper just as bad as them. After he made a round of the room, he returned to the female demon who'd lead this silly revenge party. Lima was still writhing on the floor where Selena had left her.

The bitch was lucky Raesean had showed up when he did or her soul would have gotten a one-way ticket to the Abyss straight into Abaddon's hands. A fate worse than death if he remembered correct from watching the King of the Abyss work.

Raesean squatted next to the female, waving his flamed hands in front of her face. Her gaze locked on to his and she whimpered at what she saw there.

"What are you doing in Fusion City Lima?" He asked.

She sucked in a breath, and Raesean could practically see her steeling her spine. "I thought it would be a nice place for a vacation. See the sights, have some food, meet some old friends."

He lowered his hands closer to her face. It was turning a bright shade of red now to match the corset that she wore.

"I'll find out, one way or another, what you were doing here, but trust me when I say it'll be easier if you tell me. Then I can send you back to the Amaryllis level in the Abyss. You can spend a few decades down there, trapped in the dark until your soul is strong enough to make a body that can return to the surface. Then you can be back to you regular old self again."

"Just send me there and be done with it," she spat.

"You're missing the point. I'll only send you there if you tell me what I want to know."

Lima laughed. "I'll never tell you. So you might as well start the torture then."

"You're right. I'll just get Selena to bing in her mirror so she can send you to her father. You know she's been looking for a gift to give him for father's day."

Lima's eyes widened, and her tongue darted out to coat her lips. She tried to push herself up, but the glass Selena slid under her skin and up her arms had done a number on the muscles and tendons.

150   D.H. GIBBS

The princess was vicious.

"Anyway, I'll see you on my next visit to Abaddon. Who know's he might even let you see your cousin. Wouldn't that be a treat?" He moved as though to stand.

"Wait," Lima said, "I'll make a deal with you."

"I'm listening,"

"Let me stay here at your side helping you run the city, and I'll tell you everything you want to know."

"That's a very lucrative deal you'd like to make. Tell me who sent you up here and I'll think about it."

Her throat bobbed as she fought the pain in her arms, pushing herself upright. "It was Belial. He sent me to avenge Alden. He was like a son to my father."

"I see," Raesean said. "Anything else you'd like to tell me?"

The muscle in Lima's jaw tightens. "I'm not telling you anything else until you agree to our deal."

"It was worth a shot," he said with a sigh. Standing, he used his flame free hand to brush imaginary lint off his suit. "I'll see you in the Abyss, Lima."

"What? Wait no!" A blue spark fell from his hands before she could say anything else, engulfing her in the hottest flame from the Abyss.

Raesean didn't wait to see her burn. Her shrieks were enough for him. He walked around the room looking for another demon that could give him more information. Demons were notorious gossips. He was sure someone else could tell him what she was unwilling to.

He found his prey trying to sneak his way out the door, dragging his useless legs behind him. Selena had really done a number on these demons in here.

"Well hello," he whispered, waving his flamed hands in front of the demon's face. "Now tell me what you know."

"The wrath," the demon whispered.

Raesean smiled as the demon trembled before him. Gosh. He'd really miss the tortured he'd met out while in the Abyss. He really must make trips back more regularly.

Getting the information that he needed hadn't taken as long as he'd thought. After he'd burned the last body, removing any trace of what happened, he left through the back exit of the building.

Raesean climbed into the back seat of his car, the leather groaning as he settled himself.

"To Selena's," Raesean said to his driver Henry. The Sacrodaemon, a type of demon that lived to serve, nodded. He turned the engine over, then eased out of the alleyway behind the building.

Raesean looked down at the sleeve of his white jacket. There was a spot of blood on it, right on the edge of the cuff. His gaze traveled over the rest of the jacket and he found other small flecks in a myriad of places.

Another suit ruined.

"Change of plans, Henry. Take me to my place first. I need to clean up."

The demon nodded again. He never spoke, never questioned, just nodded and followed his orders. It was why he'd hired him for this position. He need someone who would remain silent on matter what he heard and who better than a demon who wouldn't speak.

The care pulled into the garage of his apartment building. "Wait here. I'll be back shortly," he ordered.

It took no time for him to let himself into his private elevator and watched the numbers climb to his condo that took up the entire floor. He didn't examine the reason he wanted to get cleaned up before he saw Selena. After all, he was the one who decided not to pursue anything further.

How could he when she was the daughter of the man he was indebted to? The man who'd saved his life in more than one and the last thing he needed was to get involved with one creature that the ruler of the Abyss would burn everything down for.

No, he wouldn't think about why he wanted to look his best before he saw her. Why the blackened muscle in his chest gave a squeeze every time she was near? He would go to her, let her know what he found out, and then they could talk about what the hell happened with her magic today.

Crossing the unfurnished living room to the bedroom, Raesean stripped off his jacket and shirt. He dumped them in the dry cleaning pile and was about to remove his pants when he heard it.

The croaking of a frog.

He turned around, following the sound back to the center of the living room where the amphibian waited patiently. Its gigantic eyes looked him over, throat swelling with each of its croaks.

Raesean brought his hell flame, tossing a spark on the frog. It went up in flames, turning to dust instantly. Smoke rose from the ashes, forming into the shape of the king of the underworld.

"You could have just called me on my cell," Raesean said, folding his arms over his bare chest.

"That's no fun," Abaddon said. His shadow form walked the circumference of the painted portal circle he used to travel to the Abyss. Abaddon took in the empty room, heavily draped curtains that covered the floor to ceiling windows. "You really should furnish this lovely apartment. It's dreary, isn't."

"Why bother. I'm hardly here, anyway. I spend most of my time at the club.'

"At least there's that. This place looks worse that a torture room in the Abyss." Abaddon tapped a finger against his chin as though he was thinking about adding his empty living room to torture souls in the Abyss.

"To what do I owe this plague visit and not a phone call?"

Abaddon lost forms of playfulness as he turned to him. The King was in his presence. "The demons are getting restless down below. They're fighting against the invisible toque around their necks, hoping to gain freedom to the surface world."

"You and I both know that many of them don't even know they meaning for freedom. They just want to thrive on the chaos they cause. I've had to increase punishment for those pushing the line."

Abaddon tugged on the sleeves of his suit jacket. "They're testing me, Raesean, and I don't want to destroy half of the demons in the Abyss because of a few rogue ones."

Raesean scrubbed a hand over his smooth chin. "What if it's not just a few rogue demons?"

Abaddon's eyes went hard. "Tell me exactly what you know."

***

Selena sat on the sofa, her hand freshly bandaged, and feet curled under her as she suffered through various channels for news of what happened. So far, nothing had been mentioned, but that didn't mean that it wouldn't be.

Her hair was still damp from the shower she'd taken earlier and the two braids she put it in dripped onto the white cami and booty shorts she'd put on.

The TV clicked as she changed the channel again.

"Anything?" Shalik asked. He settled himself on the other end of the sofa in black sweats and a sleeveless t-shirt.

"No," Selena muttered, still pissed at him. It was because of him they were in this mess. If word got out about her magic, she was going to have to pack up and move or else every being that wanted to use her magic would soon knock on her door.

Shalik sighed, and Selena continued to ignore him.

"You have every right to be mad at me."

She slammed the remote down on the glass coffee table in front of them. "What exactly should I be mad about Shalik?

That you broke the rules and took an interview over the phone. We decided to use the vestibule for our own safety. You just threw that rule away because once again you couldn't think straight because you were under the influence of whatever potion you cooked up."

"I made a mistake. It was a hard day, and I needed something to help me through. I'm sorry, and I promise it won't happen again."

"You're sorry? Do you understand that if what happened today gets out, I'm going to have to return to the Abyss? Worse, we could have been killed and heading there right now? You promised me you were going to get help, and you lasted a week."

"What do you want from me? I told you I was sorry and it won't happen again." Shalik snapped.

"I know it won't because I can't trust you to manage the club or our business like we used to, and I think it's time I just shut everything down."

Shalik's eyes widened. "But you love Valaris. It was your dream ever since you came to Fusion City."

"Yeah, well, I guess that dreamed died along with everyone else last year."

Before Shalik could answer, there was a knock at the door. Selena already knew who it was, pushed to her feet. Everyone else would have had to wait for her to come down to the side entrance that lead to directly to her apartment or to the front of the club, but not Raesean.

She yanked the door open, to a well dress Raesean standing there with every hair in place and his hands in his pockets. She wondered if anything ever ruffled him.

His gaze traveled down her legs and back up to her eyes, face remaining carefully blank.

"Is this a bad time?" He asked.

She rolled her eyes at him, then turned and walked back to the living room. She thought she heard a hiss of breath, but didn't bother to investigate. Whatever his problem was, it was his problem. All she wanted to know was if she needed to pack.

The door slammed close behind her. Raesean's foot falls when from loud on the tile in the entryway to cushioned on the carpet in the living room.

He unbuttoned his jacket and took a seat on one of the sofa's matching arm chairs. Selena plopped down on the sofa where she was before, while Raesean settled himself on his 'throne'.

"What happened?" He demanded.

"They hired us to do a part for a teenage dryad. Turns out that teenage dryads look a lot like rogue demons trying to kill me for the death and torture of the cousin."

Raesean blinked at her flippant response before taking a deep breath. "I thought you could read beings better than this?"

"I can," Selena said, struggling not to look at Shalik.

"So how did Lima trick you into believing they were dryads?"

"It was my fault," Shalik butted in. "I took the interview via phone, even though I knew it was a risk."

"I see," Raesean said, but Selena could have sown she smelled traces of sulfur from the fire he produced. "Shalik. Can you give me a minute to talk to Selena alone?"

Shalik looked to Selena, and she jerked her chin. Shalik stood without a word and moved to the kitchen. Only when she heard him puttering about with the kettle and mugs did she turn back to Raesean.

"What's wrong," Selena whispered. "Were we seen?"

"No, and I took care of everything else so that the only thing that remained in that room are piles of ash."

Selena breathed a sigh of relief. "Then why does your face look like the world is ending?"

He moved, so he was sitting next to her on the sofa.

"Abaddon contacted me tonight."

Selena tried to jump to her feet, but Raesean grabbed her arm to keep her still. "He wants you to return to the Abyss because you're in danger up here."

"What?" she snapped.

"The rogue demons that came topside aren't just looking to get away from your father. They are working with Belial. He leads the biggest demon army in the Abyss and Alden, his nephew, was like a son to him. He wants revenge, but more importantly, he wants to overthrow your father. You are the ticket to him getting what he wants."

"He's not blood. They would never let him rule." Selena pointed out.

"Yes, but that's not stopping him from trying."

Selena whipped a why a drop of water that fell from her hair onto her thigh, while she turned Raesean's words over. When she looked back at him, his gaze was following the motion. She cleared her throat, and he looked up into her eyes, shifting so that there was more space between them.

She fought the twinge of disappointment she felt. "What does that mean for me? Should I just lie low until the whole thing blows over?"

"Your not getting it Selena. Abaddon will not leave you unprotected in Fusion City, where any being can get to you."

Selena's stomach sank because she knew exactly what Raesean was going to say next.

"He sent me to collect you, your friend and your little dog, too."

What happens when the mirror witch Selena takes a quick trip to the underworld to see the king of the underworld, with uncontrollable magic and the chemistry between her and Raesean lights up? Find out in Mirror Witch Demon

Want more to slow burn, action fantasy? Sign up for my newsletter on dhgibbs.com to get a never published exclusive read!

More from D.H. Gibbs

Lost Thrones Series
Crown By Blood (Free Prequel)
Queen By Blood (Book 1)
Alpha by Blood (Book 2)
Heir by Blood (Book 3)

Kidnapped and taken to a secret island where Nika's forced to give up the freedom she desperately wants to protect a race on the brink of extinction. Made extinct by the brother she didn't know she had. As the immortal queen, she has no choice but to take her brother's life and claim all the thrones if he doesn't kill her first. Who will survive the fight between the siblings? Or will their rivalry lead to the very war their mother tried to avoid centuries ago?

About the author

D.H. Gibbs is a USA Today Bestselling Author and Newsday T&T Choice finalist. She enjoys writing fantasy, contemporary romance, and children's books. When not navigating the adventures of her kick-ass female leads, she's a complete Starbucks and book addict who binge-watches TV series like Lucifer, Carnival Row, and Warrior. A Trinidadian native, she currently lives and creates new worlds in Japan.

For exclusive reads, updates and sneak peeks about her real-life shenanigans, subscribe to her newsletter.
https://dhgibbs.com/newsletters/
Find out more about D.H. Gibbs books on www. dhgibbs. com

Be Social with me